Advance Acclaim for *A Christmas Gift for Rose*

"Tricia Goyer's *A Christmas Gift for Rose* is a heartwarming story of faith, family, and community. Her characters and descriptions are captivating, bringing the story to life with the turn of every page."

— Amy Clipston, best-selling author of the Kauffman Amish Bakery Series

"Goyer's heartwarming, glowing tale of hope quickly captured my attention and embraced it until the last page."

— Sherry Gore, author of *Simply Delicious Amish Cooking* and editor-in-chief of *Cooking & Such* magazine

"Thoughtfully written, *A Christmas Gift for Rose* will touch the heart of every mother and daughter. A story of a young woman fearful of her future learns of her mysterious past and through this adversity finds the true path for her life. The rich Amish history is compelling. By the end of the book, the reader will want more and more of the same."

— Elizabeth Byler Younts, author of Amish historical *Promise to Return*

Also by Tricia Goyer

The Memory Jar

The Promise Box

A Christmas Gift for Rose

TRICIA GOYER

ZONDERVAN.com/
AUTHORTRACKER
follow your favorite authors

We want to hear from you. Please send your comments about this book to us in care of zreview@zondervan.com. Thank you.

ZONDERVAN

A Christmas Gift for Rose

This title is also available as a Zondervan ebook. Visit www.zondervan.com/ebooks.

This title is also available in a Zondervan audio edition. Visit www.zondervan.fm.

Requests for information should be addressed to:

Zondervan, Grand Rapids, Michigan 49530

Library of Congress Cataloging-in-Publication Data

Goyer, Tricia.
A Christmas gift for Rose / Tricia Goyer.
pages cm
ISBN 978-0-310-33678-5 (trade paper)
1. Gifts—Fiction. 2. Christmas stories. I. Title.
PS3607.O94C57 2013
813'.6—dc23 2013009649

All Scripture quotations are taken from the King James Version of the Bible.

Interior design: Walter Petrie

Printed in the United States of America

13 14 15 16 17 18/RRD/ 20 19 18 17 16 15 14 13 12 11 10 9 8 7 6 5 4 3 2 1

Iabella Rose and Casey James, Daddy and I are so thankful that God gave us both of you through adoption. You are our favorite Christmas gifts.

God setteth the solitary in families:
he bringeth out those which are bound with chains:
but the rebellious dwell in a dry land.

Psalm 68:6

One

November 1945

Rose Yoder had hoped the last rays of evening light would fight harder against the building storm clouds, but the sky was dark as she stepped from the shelter of the barn doors with milk bucket in hand. A gentle breeze stirred particles of dust and chaff. Somewhere in the distance an automobile's motor could be heard, chugging down the gravel road beyond the farm. Golden light glowed from the lantern hanging in the kitchen window, marking her way over the frozen snow, but the light didn't penetrate far enough. She struggled forward, leaving earthy smells behind her, trusting her heart to find the way to the front door when her steps weren't sure.

Was there certainty anywhere these days? No, especially not deep in Rose's heart.

Jonathan and I should be married by now . . . maybe with a boppli *on the way.*

She pushed that thought from her mind and shook her head, her breath freezing in the air. That wouldn't happen now. Not after what he'd done. Joining the military. Traveling overseas. And to think he'd had the nerve to return to their small Amish community and don his Amish garb like nothing had happened—like he hadn't shamed their community, shamed her.

"I'll be back in Berlin before Christmas, Rose. Let's not wait until next harvest to get married." His last letter had contained those words. But tomorrow was Thanksgiving Day, and he'd already been here a week. Maybe to say good-bye to his family once and for all before leaving for good. And after their last conversation, she didn't imagine she'd get a good-bye when he did.

Rose's lower lip trembled. She doubted he'd even come see her. Why would he? She'd stated plainly that things were over between them. After all, how could she give her heart fully to someone who promised her a good Amish life and then turned to the world? The Second World War had taken so much from their country—from their community. But Rose's soul felt as if it was a personal attack on her. On her dreams. On her future.

During the war, their town had changed the pronunciation of its name. *Burr-lin*, the locals practiced saying. And she'd done her own practicing: *"I don't love you, Jonathan. Not now. Not ever."* If only her feelings agreed with her words.

A cold wind stirred her *kapp* strings. Rose quickened her steps, careful not to slosh any of the steaming milk from the bucket. Mem needed every drop for the shoofly pie, Rose's favorite. Tomorrow was their Thanksgiving meal and all of the family would be gathered. So why did it feel as if the bucket weighed a hundred pounds?

The darkness pressed in, and she sucked in a cold breath. Her foot slipped slightly on the layer of ice under the snow. She adjusted her gait, saving herself from a tumble. The farm was buried under a layer of snow. Even the birdhouse, set on a high pole, was covered with a thin layer, its emptiness magnifying her ache.

Something else nagged at her, an unknown angst that twisted her gut. The same anxiety visited her every year at this time, but like a morning shadow it never fully revealed itself. There was something she needed to do, wasn't there? Something she needed to remember . . . But for the life of her she couldn't think what.

A cold wind nipped at her nose, and with her free hand Rose tucked her scarf tight under her chin. She slowly walked up the wooden porch steps, telling herself she wouldn't let the stones in the pit of her stomach keep her from enjoying her family—her dat, mem, and the younger siblings still at home. If she had nothing else, they were enough. It was a good Amish life, one she wouldn't trade for anything.

Rose opened the door and stepped through. A wall of warmth and the scent of fresh bread and lentil soup greeted her. Those smells mixed with Mem's baking, the fragrance of dried apples and pies, and the wet clothes drying on a line strung up behind the woodstove.

Two steps in, someone rose from the wooden rocking

chair near the fire and turned. Her brother's round face, dark brown eyes, and new beard greeted her.

"Marcus!" A smile filled her face. After she'd met Jonathan three years ago, and with their care for each other growing so quickly, Rose had thought she'd marry before Marcus. But the war—Jonathan's choice—changed that. Marcus had taken her spot, marrying Katie just last month. It was good to have him visit. Rose had missed him. And tomorrow her sister Vera—older by less than a year—would arrive with her husband and son.

Her older brother reached down and took the heavy milk bucket from her hand. "Rose, I could have done that. I would have liked to greet ole Bess yet."

She smiled at the release of her burden. "Oh, you're jest trying to tickle me happy so I'll make you an apple cake."

"I haven't had one in months. It wouldn't hurt yer *bruder* to try now, would it?" Tenderness filled his gaze. Even though Rose had seven other siblings, two-years-older Marcus had always been her favorite. He watched out for her. He treated her as if she needed caring for. She'd never minded.

"I cut boughs for you from my property." He pointed to a burlap sack near the door with fresh greenery spilling out. The scent of pine widened her smile. "I know how you love to decorate the windowsills, much to Dat's dismay," he added.

Rose nodded, but knew she'd see a glimmer of appreciation in Dat's gaze once she'd finished decorating. As an

Amish preacher, he lived up to the standard of the Plain lifestyle, but for some reason he had grace with Rose's desire for simple touches of beauty around their home.

"Thank you. Now where's that bride?" Rose glanced around, noting his wife, Katie, in the kitchen with Mem. A dozen pie shells lined the countertop in two rows, waiting to be filled. Katie tucked a spoon under the lid of a jar of cherries and pressed upward, breaking the seal.

"It looks like you're making a dozen more pies yet?" Rose took off her coat and scarf and hung it by the back door. "Need help?" She washed her hands in a basin of cool water.

"You can roll out those crusts." Mem's fists kneaded a mass of bread dough. "Or start on those dishes. But change your apron, Rose, please. You jest came from the barn."

Rose glanced down at her blue dress and apron—the exact style and color as her mem and sisters.

Laughter rose from her cluster of brothers and sisters in the living room as they played jacks. Elizabeth, who was in her last year of schooling, sat watching them as she spun wool. Only five-year-old Louisa stayed in the kitchen to watch.

Rose turned to her youngest sister, whose hair was as dark as the sky outside. "Louisa, would you be a dear and grab a clean apron for me? It's in the trunk."

"*Ja!*" At five, Louisa loved helping out. It made her feel older when she could be a part of the bustle and not treated like a baby, even though she was the youngest.

Mem removed an apple pie from the woodstove and placed it on the cooling rack.

"I made extra pies to share with our neighbors." She tucked a strand of gray hair back into her *kapp*, leaving a spot of flour at her temple. "I was wondering, Rose, if tomorrow you could take two pies over to Mr. and Mrs. Ault, before everyone arrives for our afternoon celebration."

Rose dipped two fingers into a jar of cherries, pulled one out, and popped it in her mouth. "*Ja*. Of course."

Katie pinched the edges of a pie crust with her fingers. "But aren't they having company—a big gathering of their own? I expected aunts, uncles, cousins to come around . . . with Harold being home and all."

Harold? Had Rose heard right? She placed a hand over her quickened heart. "He's home?"

How many times had her family prayed for their neighbor's safe return? He'd been fighting on some island in the South Pacific and had been injured. For the first few months she'd asked Mrs. Ault about news of her only son every time she saw her. But when no word came Rose held in her concern. The unknowing—the fears—had been evident in Mrs. Ault's eyes.

Rose glanced out the window in the direction of their neighbors' farmhouse. She could barely see the glow of their electric light on the front porch. Surely if things were *gut* Harold would have stopped by. What type of injury did he have? Had he lost an arm or a leg like a few other soldiers from their town?

She swallowed hard, thinking once again of Jonathan, of all he had seen as a medic. More than he'd expected to, she supposed. How could she ever truly trust her heart to someone like that, after all he'd done—all he'd seen? He'd left their community behind. He'd lived among the *Englisch*. He'd received military training. He'd worn a uniform, confirming who his allegiance was to. To be Amish meant to be a member of a community of fellow followers of God. Jonathan had walked away from that community and aligned himself to the military. Turning his back on her in the process.

How could Jonathan return and commit himself to being fully Amish after that? And how could she commit her heart to someone who'd made such a choice?

Rose removed her soiled apron. Many thought that the Second World War hadn't had much impact on the Amish of Ohio, but they couldn't be more wrong.

"Harold *is* home." Mem's words were flat. "I stopped by the Aults' house a few days ago. I had extra eggs . . ." Her words trailed off.

What was Mem not telling them?

Rose glanced around at her younger siblings. They'd stilled their play to listen, but she knew Mem wouldn't reveal whatever sad news her gaze hinted at. Mem rarely spoke of things that pained her heart. Dat said it was because her tears—which came too easily—embarrassed her.

Rose's stomach knotted as she considered going over there. "I'm sure it's *gut* to have him home, whatever the condition." She tried to sound convincing. Would seeing her childhood friend break her heart?

Did Jonathan know Harold was back? Since he'd just arrived back in town, Rose doubted it. Still, she imagined Jonathan's concerned gaze. He wouldn't be fearful of what he'd see. He'd seen it all, hadn't he? Not that she'd ask him.

Rose couldn't get Jonathan off her mind. He'd captured a large slice of her thoughts since that first evening three years ago when he'd stared at her over the fire pit at the Yoders' place during a Singing. Distance had not lessened her care.

When he'd gone overseas, Jonathan had written and told her he worked at the hospitals away from the front lines. Rose should have been thankful, but as a pacifist he should have had *no* part in supporting the war—not even in the hospitals. If Jonathan had been drafted, that would have been one thing, but he'd *volunteered*. And while other young Amish men waited out the war on the home front, growing gardens in the small county prisons or working for the Conservation Corps, Jonathan had left their Amish community and traveled to a distant country with armed soldiers. He'd trained in their camps and made friends with outsiders. The shame! And she was the one left to see the disapproval in the gazes of her fellow Amish. To hear the women's comments around the sewing circle. She was the one who'd received a visit from a very unhappy bishop upon the discovery of what Jonathan had done and where he'd gone.

"Pretty soon he's going to stop being Amish. Most likely he's already made that choice," the bishop had commented after it

was discovered that Jonathan was in France. His disapproval had been clear. Though they were friendly with their *Englisch* neighbors, there was a dividing line. Though invisible, the barrier was all Rose had been raised to know. There was "them" and "us." Rose knew there was no middle ground.

Being among the *Englisch* had no doubt changed Jonathan. Supporting the war most likely did too. In all their months apart her feelings for him had never waned, yet how could she continue loving someone who had chosen to follow the world's way?

Rose stepped forward and ladled water from the warming reservoir on the stove, preparing to set to work on the endless pile of dishes. Steam rose and fog condensed on the window above the kitchen sink. The glass reflected Louisa's approach.

"I found this apron in Mem's trunk, Rose. It even has your name on it!"

Rose flicked the water from her fingers and turned.

Mem's wooden spoon clattered to the floor. "No!" The word burst from her lips. Faster than Rose had ever seen her move, she snatched the flour-sack apron from Louisa's hand, gripping it with taloned fingers.

Katie chuckled. "It appears someone found your Christmas present—a fancy *Englisch* apron nonetheless. Only *you* would be given such a pretty gift."

A present? Rose looked at Louisa's wide-eyed shock and trembling lower lip, then turned to Mem's face. What she saw had her stepping back, pressing herself against the counter behind her. Wetness seeped through her dress at the small of her back, but she gave it no mind. A dozen questions fought for answers, but only two reigned.

Why did Mem have a look of sheer terror in her gaze as she clutched that *Englisch* apron tightly to her chest?

And what is my *name doing on it?*

Two

THE LUMBER WAGON CREAKED AND GROANED. JONATHAN Fisher held the reins with his right hand and blew warm breath into his left mitten. Winter had taken hold. A black cape of ice-rimmed darkness draped over the countryside, reminding him of the frozen Belgian woods. Had it really only been a year ago he'd tramped through the waist-high snow as they set up their field hospital during the Battle of the Bulge?

It seemed a lifetime had passed since he'd been in those foreign woods. Jonathan closed his eyes, but he couldn't block out the memory of fresh red blood dripping onto the white snow. Ambulance drivers had carried litters filled with injured soldiers to overcrowded tents that echoed with moans. He'd done his best. He'd offered prayers along with his skill, but it was not enough for some. Never enough.

His stomach tightened, but not only from the cold. Up ahead was the Yoder farm. Before the war, on his lumber runs, he'd driven by the farm with excitement, hoping to get a glimpse of Rose—his bride to be. And now? Now he feared she'd be outside, finishing up chores when he passed.

Why did I come this way again? Am I trying to punish myself?

It was hard enough that she'd told him she had no desire to marry him. Worse was knowing she turned away, ignoring his presence, when he was close. Jonathan had even attended church in the neighboring community of Charm for that very reason. His heart split in two at the disdain in her gaze, the turn of her back.

He stared ahead as he passed the house, refusing to look through the windows hoping to catch a glimpse of her. Then, in the dark night, something caught his eye to the right of the road. A shape. A huddled form. Then movement of digging.

Was that a person?

"Whoa." Jonathan pulled back on the reins and jumped down from the lumber wagon. He took a step forward. Even in the dim light he could see it was a man, lying down, propped up on his elbows and peering over a snow drift. Jonathan looked down the road in the direction of the Ault place. What was the man looking at? He hadn't moved and didn't seem concerned about the approach of the wagon and horse.

Jonathan hurried forward. The man was ill prepared for this weather, dressed in only pajama pants and a thin cotton shirt. "Hullo?" What else could he say? Was this man mad?

The man looked back. His short cropped hair stuck up from a sweaty brow. Even in the dimness, the whites of his eyes glowed, widening in horror. The man didn't speak, but motioned for Jonathan to get down. Jonathan instinctively hunkered over. He again glanced down the snow-covered road. Was something out there?

Only silence met his ears, and he saw nothing but the ruts in the snow where another wagon or buggy had passed earlier in the day.

"What is it?" Jonathan slipped to the man's side, kneeling in the snow. "Are you okay?"

"The Japs . . ." The man's words came out as a hiss. "They'll see you." He lowered his gaze. "The Japs killed them . . . killed them all. I was the only one to escape."

Pain pounded in Jonathan's heart. A lump grew in his throat. Though he tried, he couldn't swallow it away. He reached his hand to the man's shoulder, but knew better and pulled it back. Instead he studied the man's terror-filled face. It was only then Jonathan recognized Harold. Even though the man was a few years older—and had gone to the *Englisch* school—Jonathan had seen him around town. Yet with his pale face and wrinkled brow the man looked twenty years older. Rose had said Harold had gone to the South Pacific. She'd been worried. So many in the town had sent up a million prayers, cried a million tears, over their sons.

That had been one of the reasons Jonathan made his decision to join the army. He had prayed for Harold and the other soldiers. And the more he'd prayed, the more he'd questioned. How could he sit and do nothing? How could he stand the accusations in the *Englisch* gazes or listen unmoved to their comments?

He'd come back whole, but the damage had already been done. He'd paid a price too.

Jonathan hunkered down, pressing himself against the

snow. *Shell shock*. He'd seen it in the field hospital. It made sense there. The injured soldiers could still hear the droning of the bombers overhead. They could hear the pounding of the big guns. But here in the still and quiet countryside, far away from any enemy?

A minute passed, then two, as Jonathan's mind scurried, trying to figure out what to do. What to say. Finally, as if the answer came from the stars, appearing from behind the thinning clouds, he knew.

"Listen." Jonathan let out a long, slow breath. "I know a place we can hide. It's safe, warm. I can find us something to eat."

Harold looked to him, his features softening. "I *am* hungry. Earlier—" His words caught in his throat. "Earlier I woke up certain I could smell my mom's cinnamon rolls baking." His voice trembled. He shook his head. "It was a dream I didn't want to wake from."

"C'mon." Jonathan rose, not thinking about the cold, the lumber load, or his horse that stood in the middle of the road, waiting. "Follow me."

Thankfully, the man did. His steps were quick, and Jonathan picked up his pace. He headed across the yard of the Ault place, and his feet sank into the snow. *Just like the sands of Iwo Jima*.

They made it to the large, open porch, and Harold took the lead. "Come." He hurried up the steps. "My mom will be happy to meet you."

When Harold glanced back, terror had been replaced

with a smile. "I know she's been praying for us . . . That's the reason we were able to make it back."

Just like that, he was different.

Jonathan nodded, unsure of what to do. The light from the electric porch light circled him. The man opened the door. Heat escaped, welcoming them in.

"Just for a few minutes, I suppose."

He entered the kitchen. A pan of cinnamon rolls—untouched—sat on the blue linoleum countertop. A woman's soft cries carried from the other room. Hearing the door open and close again, an elderly man hurried in. His eyes were red, his cheeks splotchy. He looked to Jonathan, eyebrows lifted. Thankfulness was clear in his gaze.

"He was jest outside." Jonathan pointed behind him toward the weathered farmhouse door. "I—I need to get going, though. I have a load of lumber to deliver."

Relief flooded the man's face. He took one of his son's pink, cold hands and pressed it between his own two. Then the older man led his son to the table, pulling out a chair for him to sit. Harold said nothing, but a look of contentment radiated from his face.

"Are you not going to ask?" Mr. Ault's voice cracked.

"No need, sir. I understand."

Mr. Ault turned. His eyebrow twitched. "Are you the one?"

Jonathan crossed his arms over his chest, realizing he was trembling. "The one?"

"The Amishman who joined the army?"

Jonathan jutted out his chin, repeating the words he'd

said every time he was asked the same question. "I—I was a medic . . . at the field hospital." He pulled his felt hat from his head and turned it over in his hands. "I never fired a weapon. Not once." He returned his hat to his head.

"Thank you, son." The man's chin trembled as he came forward. He took Jonathan's hand, clinging to it for a moment. Respect radiated from his gaze. Then Mr. Ault released Jonathan's hand, stepped forward, and opened the door.

The air was cold, but warmth grew in Jonathan's chest. Did the man thank him for bringing back his son? For serving?

Jonathan squared his shoulders as he walked back to his wagon with quickened steps. He had a feeling it was both.

As he climbed back into the wagon, he couldn't help but look in the direction of the Yoder farm. The kitchen window was fogged up, and he couldn't see inside. He was glad for that. Glad Rose couldn't look out and find him there. What Jonathan had seen tonight with Harold was evidence of what he felt inside. Would returning to normal life—whole mind and heart—be possible?

Maybe Rose was right. Maybe it was hopeless to even try.

Three

THE DISHES DONE, ROSE DRIED THEM AND SET THEM IN their places in the open cupboards. The kitchen window was fogged, and she instinctively lifted her dishtowel and wiped away the condensation. In the light of the moon—which had found a way to peek through the clouds—she spotted a lumber wagon parked on the road not far from the Ault place. Rose placed a hand to her throat. Was something wrong?

Before she had a chance to alert her brother and father, she noticed a figure jogging from the Ault house to the wagon. A familiar form. Her heart quickened as she wondered if it was Jonathan. She leaned closer, trying to get a better look, but couldn't be sure.

With a slow movement, the wagon started down the road. Away from her house. Away from her.

Rose thought about the letter she'd received after Jonathan had left. He'd made his intentions clear. He'd written and said he wanted to marry her when he returned.

The postmark had been from France. Her face heated—flamed with anger even now.

"Rose?" Mem approached, placing a soft hand on her arm. "Are—are you all right? Your face looks a little flushed."

"It does?" Rose placed the dishcloth on the kitchen table and patted her cheek. "I'm . . . fine."

The children, including Louisa, were getting dressed in their bed clothes, and the room had quieted.

"If you are thinking about the apron . . ."

"The apron?" Rose hadn't been thinking about it. Not really. Why would something like that matter when her heart ached, knowing that the person she loved was close, but she couldn't bring him closer?

The wagon disappeared over the hill, and she turned back to her mem. "I wasn't thinking about the apron."

The relief on her mother's face was clear. Mem lowered her gaze and blinked away a hint of tears.

But *should* Rose be thinking about it? What had Mem bothered so? Rose watched as she moved to her rocker near the woodstove and sat with a heaviness that wasn't typical.

Except for the smoky brown of Mem's eyes—which age had partly hidden behind heavy lids—there was nothing extraordinary about her mother's face. Her cheeks were round, and her large dimples had stretched into thick lines down to her chin. Only an inch of hair—now more gray than black—peeked out in the space between her forehead and her *kapp*. Her lips were full. They were usually happy and curled upward, but not tonight. Mem's lips were pursed tight, as if there was a secret she attempted to hold in.

But there was no secret, was there? How could there

be? Mem simply wasn't the type to hold one. She had lived within these same walls since she'd married Dat twenty-five years ago. She served her family and community without a moment's rest. To Rose she was the symbol of home, and all seemed well in life when Mem was somewhere within the same walls, humming while she set to work at her chores. But there was no humming tonight. For some reason there was no peace.

Rose folded the kitchen towel and set it on the countertop.

"I think I'll head to my room. Do you mind if I take a lantern?" She looked to Dat, who sat in his rocker, whittling a piece of wood. Her dad usually resisted. He liked the family to spend time together in the common areas. What did one want to do alone that he or she couldn't do in a group?

Dat must have seen something—weariness, or worry, maybe—etched in her face. "*Ja*, but make sure you turn off the lantern before going to sleep."

"I know, I know." She hurried over to him and placed her hand on his shoulder. She wanted to place a kiss on his cheek like she'd seen *Englisch* girls do with their dats, but that just wasn't the Amish way. Love was expressed by many means throughout the day through service and care, not through physical contact. Although that didn't mean Rose didn't want a hug sometimes, or a pat on her head. Even though Rose was nearly twenty, there were times she still felt like a young child inside, wishing she could climb onto her dat's lap, letting the worries of this world fade away with the gentle rocking of his chair.

The lantern light brightened her steps, and she entered her room, closing her door behind her. How come she couldn't get Jonathan off her mind tonight? Was she second-guessing her decision? No, she couldn't do that. Not if she wanted to remain an upright church member.

She set the lantern on her side table and moved to her trunk, pushing aside her clothes and bedding to reach the small box tucked in the bottom right corner. She opened it and pulled out the letter on top. The letter that had changed everything.

Dear Rose,

I didn't want to tell you when I left exactly where I was going. I was afraid you'd try to talk me out of it. I was certain that with one look from your blue eyes you could talk me into anything. Or talk me out of anything.

The truth is that I wasn't drafted after all. Everyone assumed I had been, and that I'd do what the other Amish young men had done before me. That I'd sit out my time in prison or join the CC. I'm not doing any of those things, Rose. You see, I chose to go. I signed up.

The paper in her hands trembled, as it had the first time she read the letter. As it did every time she read the letter.

I know you wonder why, Rose. How could I join the military when they are against everything we believe in as pacifists? Just so you know, I will not carry a weapon. I could never fire a weapon at a person knowing that my deed could send someone to eternal damnation. May it be God's hand—not mine—that causes our enemies to breathe their last. May He have mercy on their souls.

Instead I'll be working in the field hospitals, caring for injured men. I've thought about it long and hard. I've prayed too. The thing that God has brought to my mind over and over is the story of the Good Samaritan. Religious leaders walked by the injured man without offering help. They crossed the street and didn't give even one sip of water—not a kind word of concern. They had dedicated their lives to God's work, yet it was the Samaritan whom Jesus praised.

Jesus told us to love our neighbors, those injured and in need. How could I sit safely on my farm knowing that many were hurt and dying? Knowing that I could cross the street—or in this case cross an ocean—to help. Should we place our religion above the care of others?

I'm writing a letter, sharing my heart beliefs with Mem and Dat too. If you could stop by soon and comfort them, I know they will need it. There are many who won't understand my choice or my reasons. I am willing to accept that.

But more than anything I hope you'll understand. I can't bear the thought of disappointing you. When I return—and I plan to return—I only want one thing, Rose: to marry you and to live a happy, peaceful life.

Please write and tell me you understand. Tell me you agree with my plan.

Forever yours,
Jonathan

Rose had written a letter, but she had not been as understanding as he hoped. She had not agreed to marry him. How could he do this, she'd asked. How could he shame himself, his family, and her? Weren't there injured men closer? Couldn't one help returning soldiers without having to join the military? To join the military was to turn one's back on being Amish. Even reading his letter—well, it sounded more like one from an *Englisch* person!

Her letter must have crossed his second one in the delivery, because his second letter told her he did not yet realize her disapproval.

Dear Rose,

In all my life I would have never imagined all the things I've seen, experienced. Just riding on a train for the first time, as I left Ohio, was quite remarkable. Then meeting men from all over the United States during my medical training. Being with these men reminded me of our Amish community. Everyone cares for the others like brothers. When one man is down, thinking of home and family, the others lift him up. (If only the cooking was as fine as that of an Amish cook, but I am adjusting.)

But even greater than seeing New York City, sailing across the Atlantic, or setting foot onto France, was seeing Paris. We arrived not long after liberation, and I know as a Plain person I shouldn't be so enamored with fine things, but even after all the destruction of the war I never thought such a place could exist. It's as if man looked at God's beautiful flowers and used stone to create arches and gateways. The buildings rise tall and white, reminding me of my farm with its first covering of fresh snow. The people are thin and war torn, but full of joy that they are no longer under German occupation. I've heard horrible stories of what they endured, and I'm already putting my medical skills to good use.

Speaking of which, I'm on duty in just a few minutes. Give your family my love.

Forever yours,
Jonathan

Tears filled Rose's eyes. She'd wished she could be happy about his news, his experiences. Part of her still wanted to be. Part of her wished she could ask him over for Thanksgiving dinner—to enjoy spending time with him. Yet if she'd learned one thing growing up, it was that one compromise led to more, and soon one would no longer be Amish. If each individual did what he or she saw fit, there would be no community and church. Soon they would be no different than the *Englisch*.

"There can only be one right way," Rose mumbled as

she folded Jonathan's letters and placed them back in the box. But even as the words escaped her, her mind wished it wasn't so.

She loved Jonathan, but confessing that to him would mean disagreeing with her bishop—the man who stood before God.

She thought back to the words of Jonathan's letter. "*I would have never imagined all the things I've seen.*" How could he stay Amish after that? Would he ever be content in Berlin? Rose expected that any day she'd hear the news that he'd left for good—not only their community, but also the Amish. And if they'd married, where would that leave her?

She couldn't imagine not being in this community, not being Amish. It would be hard enough moving into her own home, leaving Mem and this place. But to risk being shunned by her family and all she knew . . . Rose couldn't bear it.

Rose returned the small box and closed the trunk. She'd removed her *kapp*, preparing to put on her sleeping handkerchief, when a knock sounded on the door. "Come in."

The door swung open and her fourteen-year-old sister Elizabeth stood there with a hand planted on her hip. "Dat asked me to check on you. I told him I thought you were sick . . . lovesick."

"You never were subtle, were you?" Rose couldn't help but chuckle.

Elizabeth neared, narrowing her gaze. She walked with heavy steps. There was nothing petite or dainty about Elizabeth. "Well, are you okay?"

"*Ja*, I'm fine. Just tired, I suppose."

Elizabeth plopped onto Rose's bed. "You say that, but it must be something more. I can see it in your eyes, Rose. You look afraid."

"No, not really. I have nothing to be afraid about." Rose bit her lip, knowing her words were a lie. She just hoped Elizabeth couldn't see it.

"Maybe not, but you've been acting different ever since Jonathan Fisher came back from the war. I wasn't joking when I told Dat you were lovesick."

Rose pulled the pins from her bun one at a time until her blonde hair spilled down her back. She refused to respond to that. What did her sister know?

"I don't know why you won't let him see you. He's driven by the last three days. He's just waiting for someone to step out onto the porch and wave him in."

Rose spun around. "He has not . . ."

Elizabeth's headed nodded enthusiastically. "*Ja*, has too. Ask Mem. Ask Louisa. Ask anyone."

"You're too young to understand."

"Marcus said you won't see him because he became a soldier."

"He didn't become a soldier. He became a *medic*."

Elizabeth fiddled with the string on her *kapp*. "Marcus said the Amish folks will soon forget about that, especially now that he's back."

"What do you know?" she stated flatly. "You didn't hear the bishop's words. You didn't see the looks that I received.

Numerous women came up to me after church services and told me that I needed to forget about Jonathan—that there were many good Amish men who would make fine husbands. Their disapproval was clear on their faces."

"I know that if any boy looked at me the way Jonathan looks at you, Rose, I wouldn't think twice about getting married. Doesn't every woman want to be loved like that?"

Without another word Elizabeth slipped from the room. What was she going to tell their dat? That the only thing wrong with Rose couldn't be fixed by anyone in this house?

Rose touched her fingertips to her cheeks. Could they really see her fear? Maybe she *was* afraid.

Afraid of where giving her whole heart would take her? *Ja.*

Afraid of where she'd end up if she turned her back to him? Yes, that was true too.

Afraid of being alone? Always.

And a new fear stirred: what was the secret Mem hid? Did she know something Rose didn't? Did Mem have an answer to the uneasy feeling that crept over Rose like the dark, foreboding shadow of an unseen truth?

Four

IT TOOK LONGER THAN NORMAL FOR JONATHAN TO tend to his horse. He moved with sluggish steps as he unhitched the animal, brushed him down, and fed and watered him. Partly because his hands were frozen. He should stop taking the long route on these lumber deliveries. He should just face the fact that his choice had ruined his chance with Rose. No matter how many times he drove by she would not be interested in seeing him.

He also carried the additional burden of seeing Harold Ault. He had not heard that the young man was back from the war, and now he knew why. How were Mr. and Mrs. Ault handling it? From what he saw, not well. Did they have hopes that their son would someday snap back?

Jonathan hung the harness on the hook on the wall. He knew better. Even if the shell shock wore off, what Harold had seen would affect him forever.

Jonathan closed his eyes and took a deep breath. The whistles of the screaming mimis were present even in the silence. The smell of gangrene and trench foot. The tearful moans of men waking without sight, without the ability to walk.

It's over, he tried to convince himself, wishing his mind and heart believed it was so.

He tightly shut the door to the warm barn and thought about his first impressions of France. He'd seen the war-torn land and rejoiced in the Nazi defeat. He'd had false hope during that first week in Paris that he'd mostly be caring for those left in war's wake. What he hadn't realized was that the Nazis had no intention of giving up so easily, and the fight called the Battle of the Bulge would be only the first of the horrors.

And what had kept him strong as he cared for the injured soldiers, most barely eighteen? Thoughts of Rose had brought strength to his weary limbs. He'd thought of her smile. Her brilliant blue eyes. He'd considered returning to her embrace.

What a fool.

Jonathan's boots tromped through the frozen snow as he hurried to his parents' house. As the youngest son, the large farmhouse would someday be his. Before he'd left to become a medic he'd even started work on the *dawdi* house in the back, where his parents would live after he married. Now it sat an empty shell. No need to get to work completing that anytime soon.

He stomped the snow from his boots and opened the door to the kitchen. His oldest sister Ruthann sat at the table next to Mem, peeling potatoes. Surprise caused him to pause. Ruthann lived more than two miles down the road. He rarely saw her during the week, and he never saw her without her six children.

"Johnny, get in, would ya? Yer letting out all the warm air," Dat called from his spot near the woodstove.

Jonathan hurried inside and hung his hat on the hook near the door. He removed his boots and placed them alongside the other shoes neatly lined on wooden shelves. Then he turned to his sister. "Did you come for a visit?"

Ruthann tossed a dishtowel his direction. "Did you forget what day tomorrow is? My Sally is caring for the little ones while Mem and I cook. Thought it would work better this way without the twins underfoot."

The twin boys were toddlers and the most active children he'd ever known.

Tomorrow. Thanksgiving. "*Ja*, of course."

Thanksgiving meant a day of gathering as a family, of enjoying a meal and having a time of Bible reading together. But before that was a time of fasting . . . of being prayerful and still before God.

Jonathan hung his jacket. He washed up in the water basin in the kitchen. It had been a long time since he'd been still before God. He spent his days living for Him; he just didn't feel too comfortable praying *to* Him much. Mostly due to shame.

During those dark nights in the Belgium woods, he should have turned to prayer, seeking God's strength to help him, instead of turning to thoughts of Rose.

He also worried. What if he prayed now and God made it clear that a life with his dear Rose would never be? Mem and Dat always said that God's way was perfect.

He didn't see how that could be in a scenario without her as his wife.

Finally, to be still was to question if he'd done the right thing by becoming a medic. At the time Jonathan had felt that's what God's Word had told him, but what if he'd been wrong? What if he'd given up everything for something that didn't matter as much as he thought?

"Son, will you fill my big pot half full with water and set it on the cookstove?" Mem asked. "You know with my arthritis I can barely lift it."

"*Ja*, of course."

Jonathan did what his mem asked, thankful Dat had agreed to let him pipe water into the house. His sister's eyes were on him as he worked.

"Did you take the longer route? Is that what took you so long?" Ruthann's voice was even, as if she was just trying to make conversation.

"It's a better road."

"*Ja*, and a better view. I think . . ."

The sound of the water hitting the metal pan dimmed her words. He waited until the pot was half full before he turned off the spigot and looked to her. "What was that?"

Ruthann sighed. "I said you shouldn't give up on Rose too easily. Every time I see her at church she looks miserable—has dark circles under her eyes. She looks as if she's lost weight too. I bet she's hardly eating and not sleeping a wink. She loves you, Jonathan. Everyone knows it's so."

"*Ja*, but does she respect me? That's something to question. Not now she doesn't."

"Who's to say her opinion can't change? With you gone it was easy for Rose to listen to the disapproval of others, but you're back now. When you were overseas they said you were going to leave the community for good. While you were gone, they said you'd be changed when you returned. But you're back. Your presence—your commitment—will silence their words. In the meantime, show Rose you still care. Be there for her. Give her time. Do something special for her. Show her yer not going anywhere. Walking around like a wounded puppy will do neither of you any good."

"You sure have a lot of advice, Ruthann."

"Haven't I always?" She glanced up at him and winked. "I may be a bossy older sister, but sometimes I do have somethin' *gut* to say."

"But what if it doesn't work? What if I reach out to Rose and she still turns her back on me?"

Ruthann set a peeled potato on the table and picked up another. "Oh, little brother, that's not the question I'd focus on. Instead I'd be thinking, *What if it does work? Ja*, it's risking yer heart, but consider jest who you are risking it for. Consider that."

Five

Rose didn't realize it was the howling of the wind that woke her until another blast hit the window, rattling in its frame. The cold November winds pounded on the glass, demanding to be let in. A howl rose—a fearful cry. Was someone outside the window calling to her?

She opened her eyes to discover she was sitting, legs swung over the side of her narrow twin bed. Stockinged feet pressed to the cold wooden floor. Someone moved beside her. A gasp escaped her lips.

"It's me, Rose." Mem's voice was soft. "I'm here."

Rose placed a hand over her pounding heart. "Is it almost morning?"

"*Ne*. I was jest falling asleep when I heard your cry. Was it a nightmare?"

Rose touched her sleeping *kapp*. "*Ja*." She blew out a sigh and then waited. She waited for what was to come next—Mem's whispered prayers. It was the only time she heard Mem—heard anyone—praying out loud. Silent blessings were the Amish tradition, but Mem must have known she needed to hear about God's promises, God's protection.

What would Rose do without her mem there for her whenever the nightmares came?

But Mem didn't pray. She just sat there silent.

How could I ever tell anyone other than Mem about my nightmares? They seemed so foolish, as if she was a young child yet.

Rose looked around. *I'm in a safe place. It was just a dream.* She reminded herself what was real. Her mother . . . this room.

She'd shared this room with her sister Vera until they reached their teen years and it was clear there wasn't enough room for two in the bed nor two to share the trunk. Now Vera was married with a baby of her own. Would Rose ever be able to claim as much?

The white walls of the bedroom appeared gray, washed out in the strands of moonbeams. Mem's face did too. Rose swiped her cheeks with the back of her hand, wiping away evidence of her tears.

The wind died down. Only silence filled the air. A sliver of moonlight slipped through the window. Rose could still see the questions in her mother's eyes.

She reached out. Mem's warm hand took hers. "Mem, are you going to pray?"

"Are you all right, Rose? I heard you crying out." Mem's voice was frigid, trembling, as if the winter wind lay trapped within her lips.

"I—I suppose."

Why didn't Mem answer her question?

A shiver traveled up Rose's spine. Her room was cold,

which meant the woodstove had died down. Even colder was the tension deep inside her gut.

Rose didn't have to wonder what she'd been dreaming about. She knew the motions of the dream as well as she knew the etched wrinkles of Mem's face.

"The nightmare is back, Mem. I don't understand."

"Is it always the same, Rose?" Mem clutched Rose's hand tighter, as if she was the one who needed reassurance.

"*Ja*. It's the same. I am away, and I come home. It's not this house, but another. A small one. I search the rooms—there are four rooms. They seem so empty."

A puddle of moonlight slipped between the thin, white curtains, and Rose strained to see her mother's face. "Do you think, Mem, that my nightmares come from fear of having my own family? It makes no sense, but I almost fear that once I do they'll be taken from me. Do you think that's yet another reason I push Jonathan away?"

Mem's mouth opened then closed again.

Rose tapped her stockinged toe on the worn wooden floor. She expected Mem to tell her that their conversation could wait until morning. She expected Mem's prayers. But still Mem was quiet.

"It's an empty house," Rose continued. "The walls are tall. Bare. There is an open window."

Mem's fingers trembled. "Is that all?"

She closed her eyes and thought back. She never wanted to remember the dream, think about it. No matter the years that passed, she always felt like a small child. A lost, sad child.

"Maybe I was looking for someone?"

"I know who you're looking for." Mem's voice quivered.

Rose leaned closer. "You?"

"*Ne*, Rose." Mem looked away. "I should have told you sooner."

"Told me what?"

Mem pulled her hands away. "In the morning."

"No." The word shot from Rose's lips. "This has to do with the secret, doesn't it? All evening you tried to hide it, but it's been clear on your face."

Mem sat still, and minutes passed. Finally she straightened her back, as if setting her resolve. "Do you remember much of your childhood, Rose?"

"*Ja*, of sharing my room with Vera. Of running around the orchards, climbing trees. I fell once and hurt my arm."

"Do you remember where you lived when you hurt your arm?"

"I jest said I shared my room with Vera."

"Rose, don't you remember? You didn't always share your room with Vera."

Rose lowered her head and folded her hands on her lap. She remembered a warm body curled up next to her. Soft breathing. The cool of the room, but warmth under the blankets. Dat's snores.

Her brow furrowed. Mem and Dat's room was at the far end of the hall on the second story. How was she able to hear her father's snores as a child?

"We didn't always live in this house? I thought we did—"

"*Ne*, Rose. Before this house we lived in a house in Charm. But . . ."

Rose waited.

"Before that there was another house you lived in." Mem pointed to the lantern on Rose's side table. Rose nodded and lit it.

Mem sighed. "I've been wondering when the perfect time to tell you was . . . I suppose now is as good a time as any."

"What do you mean?"

"There's something I need to talk to you about. Something important." Mem fidgeted and then focused on Rose's eyes. "Do you remember Christmas 1932?"

Rose shook her head. "*Ne*. I was only four. I hardly remember anything from back then."

"Wait right here."

Mem took the lantern, and Rose could hear her walking up to her room. The squeaks of the stairs were more pronounced in the dead of night. A minute later she returned with a note written along the edge of newsprint. The newspaper was yellowed, and the date on the paper was 1932.

Rose read the words out loud:

> Mary, we love Rose more than she'll ever know. We love her so much we are choosing life for her. To hear her crying herself to sleep at night with an empty stomach breaks our hearts. We're moving on to find work in California. We know in your home she'll be loved and

fed . . . both physically and spiritually. Leaving is the hardest thing we've ever done. Betty.

The paper quivered in Rose's hand. And her mind took her back to a small green kitchen table. The faces were barely visible in the low candlelight. An *Englisch* man and woman. Boys. A baby.

The boys . . . a baby . . . Betty. Rose placed a hand over her stomach. It clenched tight. "In my mind there is an image of a family. An *Englisch* family. Sometimes they are in my dreams too. But not the nightmares. They are in my happy dreams. Are you telling me they are real?"

"*Ja*, Rose. When we lived in Charm, Stan and Betty were our *Englisch* neighbors. They were a good family but the Depression hit them hard. They did their best to care for their children, but there wasn't enough food. Your father's heart must have ached to feel the thin skin over your frail bones."

Mem lifted her hand to Rose's cheek. "And our neighbors—they never asked for handouts, but we noticed something. As it neared mealtime, usually lunch or dinner, you would show up at our front door. You told us your mama sent you to play, but we knew better." Mem chuckled softly. "You ate so much for a little thing, and after a while you were starting to look healthier . . . But that wasn't the case with your sister." Mem lowered her head. "She was a plump, healthy baby, but . . ."

"Did something happen to her?"

Mem nodded. "Your parents did what they could, but

it was a hard winter. Too hard. She slipped away and broke everyone's heart."

Rose tried to make sense of what Mem was saying. Another mother. A sister—Rose's sister—who had died. It was something to be sad about, she knew. But it was too much. These words that Mem spoke were harder to understand than the unsettled feelings. It was harder to understand than the nightmare.

"Then what happened after . . . my sister . . . died?"

"Things didn't get better. The jobs were few. The storms came. The banks . . . Well, even those who had reserve funds lost them." Mem sighed. "And then you became sick. There were days I'd watch for you, and when I saw you coming down the road I'd run to you, wrap you up in a blanket, and bring you into the house. Some mornings I woke worried that you'd be too weak to come down the road that day."

Rose tried to process what Mem was saying. Part of her felt that her mother's story was the dream, but another part believed the truth of Mem's words deep down inside. It made sense. The sense of missing something . . . of a longing that was unexplained. As the words seeped in, her child's heart ached for the family she'd once had.

"And what happened?" Rose was almost fearful to ask. "What happened to that family?"

"One day when you came over to help with the Christmas baking, yer daddy never came for you, like he usually did. I asked Marcus to walk you back. I couldn't leave the other children, and Dat was in the barn choring. You looked so small as Marcus led you with the lantern. I watched at the window. Fifteen minutes passed, twenty. Your father—Dat—came in, and I urged him to go look for you and Marcus. He was putting his boots back on when I saw the lantern. Marcus was nearly dragging you down the road. He said your family was gone." Tears filled Mem's eyes. "Marcus said the house w-was e-empty." Her words came out broken. "He said you kept running from room to room looking for your family . . . and that he had to bribe you to leave. He told you Dat would give you a pony ride if you walked back with him."

Rose's mouth felt dry. Her eyes did too. Mem's words hung above her heart, unable to penetrate.

"Your dat and I went and checked. Marcus was right. The—your—family was gone. The only thing left was this note and a small package."

The trembling started in Rose's arms and moved through the rest of her body. "I—I don't feel so good." Cold enveloped her, and she motioned for Mem to rise. Mem moved to the trunk, sitting upon it. Rose watched her. She expected Mem to cry. Mem always cried over things far less than this. Instead Mem's face carried a serene look, as if a great burden had lifted from her shoulders.

"It must have been hard . . . keeping that secret for so long." Rose wasn't sure if she'd said the words out loud.

Then—as if her grandmother's quilt could protect her from the rest of the story—Rose climbed underneath it until only her eyes and nose peeked out.

It's not my grandmother's quilt. This isn't my family, my home. My mem . . . my dat. Everything she knew was a lie. They'd taken pity on her. Pity.

The wind picked up again, and her thoughts pounded even stronger.

"I'm so sorry I didn't tell you sooner." Mem's voice was just a whisper. "I—I suppose we can talk more tomorrow . . . after everyone leaves."

Thanksgiving. Rose's stomach plummeted. What did she have to be thankful for? First, she'd lost Jonathan, and now her family too? The truth—others' choices—had stripped her of both.

What's left? Will everything be taken away?

Mem opened her arms, but Rose pulled back. Mem hadn't hugged her often in recent years, and the times she had were times of loss. But even Mem's hugs couldn't help her now.

Rose saw the pain in her mother's face as she pulled away. Mem hesitated, then dimmed the lantern and stood. Rose wanted to speak to her. To ask her to stay. But what right did she have to do that? Her lower lip trembled.

Mem slipped from the room, and Rose turned to her side and tucked her knees to her chest, hoping to retain her warmth. A chill seeped through the glass window. Or maybe it came from within. Soon nothing moved within the house, and the only sound outside was the creak of the chain of the porch swing as it shifted. Her thoughts filled the void. Were her parents still alive? Her brothers? Where did they end up? Had things worked out for them? Had things been easier with one less mouth to feed?

Tomorrow morning everyone else would wake up as if nothing had happened. But everything had changed. How was she going to face the day? Face the people she knew as well as she knew herself?

Actually, they knew her better. Marcus knew the truth. Did Vera too?

She'd never felt as alone as she did at this moment. Here, but not belonging. Here, but only because they didn't have a choice.

Who else knew the truth? What about all those at church? She lay there a moment. Despite her fatigue she couldn't keep her mind from racing. Finally she rose and pulled on another pair of knitted socks, wrapped the blanket around her shoulders, and peered out the window. Would she ever feel warm again?

Blue moonlight draped over the barn and yard. Behind the barn was Dat's field. And somewhere in Charm stood her real parents' small shack. Had she ever passed it as they visited friends and family in that area? How could she not have known? How could she not have remembered?

Rose wiped her nose on the sleeve of her night dress. She thought of sitting on her dat's lap as a child, by the fire as he went through the Scriptures. He'd never speak out loud but his lips moved as he read, and sometimes she recognized a word. Had she ever sat in the lap of her real father like that? Mem said his heart must have ached to feel thin skin over her frail bones.

She thought of the family again, pressing her eyes tight

and trying to picture their faces and their clothes—*Englisch* clothes.

Then, as if every star came crashing down, every speck of light dimmed around her.

"My *Englisch* parents," Rose whispered. "I'm . . . *Englisch*."

Six

THE HOUSE WAS QUIET. TOO QUIET. JONATHAN'S SISTERS and their families wouldn't be arriving until later. Yet he knew that even in the middle of the busyness his sisters wouldn't leave him alone. He was the only one not married, and even before he'd decided that he wanted to marry Rose they'd declared her to be the perfect woman for him. Maybe it was her sweet, gentle nature. Maybe it was because of the way she cared for her younger brother and sisters. Maybe it was because she cared about this community. To Jonathan, she maybe cared about the community too much—at least about their opinions.

He sat at the kitchen table with his Bible open before him. His father had been silent, sitting on the other end reading and praying. His mother had been in her room, most likely doing the same. The solemn day would soon slip into a joyous one, but it felt far from joyous without Rose. While he was overseas, he'd counted down the days until he could see her again. This—this wall between them—made all the eager waiting seem like a horrible joke.

Jonathan flipped through the pages of the Bible wishing

he'd spent more time in prayer while he was away, instead of just focusing on thoughts of Rose. Perhaps he'd done it because it had been easier thinking of a future with her than considering the present. It was hard to see the soldiers dying and think of God. It had been hard to see the concentration camps and wondering why God hadn't done more to stop it all.

"It just proves that sin will have its mark on us until we can be with God for eternity," his bunkmate Roy Wilburson had told him.

Jonathan's dad cleared his throat, and Jonathan jumped slightly. Maybe Rose should be worried. Maybe the war had affected him more than he wanted to let on.

With a creak of the hallway door, his mem bustled into the kitchen. She hummed softly. Jonathan envied her attitude that always saw the bright side of everything.

"Jonathan, I have an errand for you to run." A smile filled her plump face, pushing up her cheeks.

Jonathan's eyebrows furrowed. "Today?"

Dat turned and glanced over his shoulder, equally surprised.

"*Ja*, during the last sewing circle Mary Yoder left her best serving dish here. It's just a mile or so to their house. I know the Yoders are having all their children, *ja*, and it would be a shame if she was missing her best dish."

"Oh, yer worried about the dish—is that it, Mem?"

She shrugged as she moved to stoke the cookstove.

"And it wouldn't hurt none to wish Rose a good day

while I'm making a delivery to her mem, now would it?" Jonathan pushed his heavy chair back from the table and rose. "And will you admit Ruthann put you up to this?"

Mem paused, placing her hands on her hips. "I won't admit any such thing." She pointed her finger. "But I will say Ruthann mentioned she won't let you back in this house unless you have a *gut* talk with that woman. A *gut* talk, Jonathan."

THE COLD OF LAST NIGHT SEEMED A DISTANT MEMORY AS the house warmed with the heat of the woodstove and the sunlight reflecting off the snow and streaming in the windows. Rose sat in Mem's rocker. The old, tattered German Bible was open on her lap, but she hadn't read a word. Actually, she'd read many words, but none of them had penetrated.

Thanksgiving morning was a time of fasting for the adults. The children had eaten a simple meal of biscuits and jam and kept mostly to their rooms, but as it neared noon, Mem rose from where she'd been sitting at the kitchen table and began pulling the food they'd prepared last night from the pantry. Children showed up from various corners of the house. The noise of Mem moving around the kitchen, adding water to the kettle to heat for tea, meant that their solemn morning would soon turn into a time of celebration. To Rose, the silence was easier than celebrating. She wanted to talk to Mem, but at the same time was afraid to know more about what had happened to her family.

She wished she could talk to Jonathan . . .

Rose's stomach cinched. Last week she'd looked Jonathan in the face and told him that she saw no future for them. Over the last few months she'd listened to the biting words of those in her community who'd been outspoken about Jonathan going against the Amish way. Last night, she'd tried to push all thoughts of him out of her mind. Yet now—in her time of need—he was the one she longed to talk to.

What a fool I've been.

Heat rose to her cheeks, considering how she'd practically shunned him for caring for *Englisch* soldiers and there she was *Englisch* herself!

Rose swallowed down her emotion and started rocking faster. Who knew if she'd ever have the chance to talk to him? If she did, she guessed Jonathan would be the one to turn his back on her now. And she wouldn't blame him if he did.

All the Amish people Rose knew had been Amish all their lives. Well, except for one—a local woman who'd fallen in love with an Amish bachelor and decided to convert. Though she tried her hardest, she never really fit in. Outsiders weren't accepted. And that's what she was. The truth declared it so. How would Rose be any different?

She glanced at the clock, realizing Vera, LeRoy, and little Ira would be there soon, in addition to Marcus and Katie. She guessed Vera knew the truth, but what about their younger siblings?

Eight-year-old Martha entered the room and twirled lightly on her toes, enjoying the greenery that Rose had set up in the windows at dawn. Martha's apron puffed slightly as she turned. "Look, Rose, I'm a snowflake, not?"

"*Ja*." Rose smiled. Martha's carefree spirit was not one to be tamed. In the summer she danced on dirt and dry grass and declared she was a dandelion seed. She whistled with the birds. If she were to know about Rose she surely would have said something. The little ones had no reason to question if Rose was a real sister. Even with her lighter hair and eyes, Rose hadn't questioned. She just believed she took after family members who were also fair.

Trying her best to hold back her tears, Rose put on her shoes and coat and then hurried to the kitchen.

Mem set a kettle of water on the woodstove to boil. She glanced up surprised. Her eyes were red, and Rose guessed she hadn't slept much either. "Going somewhere?"

"To the Aults, remember? To take the pies."

"Oh, *ja*. I'd forgotten . . . Or I can ask Elizabeth."

"*Ne*." Rose chose an apple pie and a cherry one. "I need some fresh air."

"*Danki*, Rose." Mem offered a sad smile. "And let them know we are praying for them, *ja*?"

Rose nodded and balanced one pie on her hand and the other on her arm as she opened the door and slipped outside. Near the barn Martha's twin brother Matthew tossed snowballs at the fence. He cheered for every one that hit the wood.

How many childhood joys had Rose taken for granted?

The air was cold, but it wasn't far to the Aults' house.

Instead of walking across the small field between their houses, the deep snow forced her to walk along the road. As she trudged along, Rose's mind was heavy with the knowledge of what Mem had told her. She was not Mem's child, not birthed from her like the other children. The ache of knowing that was enough, but even greater was the ache of realizing that she had another family . . . an *Englisch* family.

"I'm . . . not . . . Amish." She pushed each word out, and each froze in the air and plunked onto the ground before her, hitting the frozen snow. The horror of the words was felt more than comprehended.

Rose paused her steps more than once, trying to keep the tears from coming. She was thankful this morning was one for fasting; she was certain she wouldn't have been able to eat more than a few bites, and even if she'd done that, she would have lost it already on the snow.

When she'd woken up, after a fitful sleep, she'd forced herself to dress, pausing when she placed her prayer *kapp* on her pinned-up blonde hair, feeling like a traitor as she did. Even the image of her blonde hair mocked her in the small hand mirror she used. Blonde hair when everyone else in the family had brown.

She should have paid more attention to it before, but Dat's sisters had blonde hair too. Many families she knew had at least one or two children who looked a bit different than the others. Now she knew the reason she did.

Her footsteps reached the driveway of the Ault place,

and she paused to catch her breath. It was only then that she saw the footprints in the snow—two sets crossing the yard.

She thought again of Jonathan. Had that been him last night? If so, was he simply making a delivery? Or did he come by regularly, as Elizabeth said?

Rose ignored the footprints and hurried up the driveway, eager to see Mr. and Mrs. Ault—to see Harold in whatever state he was in—and then escape to her room for a few minutes of quiet before everyone else arrived. She'd tried to pray this morning, but the words didn't come. Maybe God knew her heart. Maybe attempting to turn to Him in her need was enough.

She moved up the porch steps. The door opened before she had a chance to knock.

"Come in, dear." Mr. Ault's voice was flat. "But make sure you keep your voice low. Harold is startled easily these days." Mr. Ault didn't explain more than that.

She nodded and entered the warm kitchen. She expected to see her friend lying on the couch, his body broken. Instead he sat at the table, looking as perfect and healthy as he'd always been.

Rose's jaw dropped, and she hastily set the pies on the Formica-topped table. In the other room a radio played an upbeat tune. If it weren't for the solemn face of Mr. Ault she'd think nothing had changed.

"Harold?"

His eyes moved to her, as if trying to recognize her . . . then he smiled. "Rose. It's you."

He didn't rise. He didn't offer a handshake or a hug, but instead took a sip from the steaming coffee cup in front of him.

Rose looked to Mr. Ault. His hair was twice as gray as she'd last seen him. Heavy bags hung under his eyes, and he said nothing. He refused to look at his son and instead busied himself, wiping down an already clean kitchen counter with a towel. Mrs. Ault entered, took the dishcloth from his hand, and then motioned to the living room.

"Why don't you go sit, dear," she said sweetly.

Her husband nodded once and then hurried from the kitchen, seemingly relieved.

"Mrs. Ault, I brought two pies. There is a cherry pie and an apple one . . . because I know apple is Harold's favorite."

"Apple pie. It sure is." He gave a low whistle. "Why don't you sit a minute and we can catch up? I won't tell you what I just experienced . . . I just got off the ship last night."

Rose's heart sunk as she suddenly understood. It wasn't his body that had been broken by the war, but his mind. And in a way this was even harder to see.

"Thank you, Harold." She pulled out the wooden chair, painted white, and sat on the red-and-white-checkered cushion.

He pointed out the window. "We docked right there . . . and there was horrible gunfire." He turned to Rose, his eyes piercing. "No, not now, I won't tell you any of that—don't want to worry you. But I will say, Rose, that thoughts of you kept me going even during times I wanted to give up."

Rose's brow furrowed, and she placed a hand over her

heart. Harold was two years older, and a nice neighbor boy, but they'd never been anything more than friends. She'd never think of dating an *Englisch*man . . .

She bit her lower lip. She couldn't quite comprehend that she was one of them—the fact she shared more with this family, in this room, than she did with the family across the field, no matter the clothes she wore.

"Harold, do you want some cream for your coffee?" his mother asked.

Rose noticed Mrs. Ault didn't offer her a cup. Didn't suggest that she stay—which was not usual. But instead of rising, Rose stayed planted in the chair. Partly because her kneecaps quivered and she worried that if she tried to stand she'd be forced to sit again. And partly because she wanted to hear what Harold had to say.

"Rose, it was awful." His words poured out. "We landed on the beach—it was black sand, but it got to be where there were more bodies covering the shore than anything else. Our landing vessel couldn't make it too close to the beach, because there were bodies in the water too. I jumped out and struggled forward. It's amazing I made it to the beach at all, my pack was so heavy. And as I lay behind a tall sand dune as my only protection, I remembered my mother's words: "*God has a way of protecting those special to Him . . . those that He rescues, just as He did in Rose's case.*"

"Rescued?" Rose looked to him, puzzled. "What do you mean by that?"

A crashing sounded, and Mrs. Ault bent over to pick

up the tin cup she'd dropped. Just as quick was the sight of Harold crashing to his knees as he covered his head. Then he glanced up, eyes wide with horror. Followed by shame.

His face lost all color, and Rose wondered if he was more horrified by his reaction or the fact she'd seen it.

Harold looked to the cup in his mother's hand. He cursed and hurried into the living room. He plunked down on the camelback sofa next to his father and lowered his head, covering his face with his hands.

"I can't believe I did that. I didn't mean to let the cup slip." The color had drained from Mrs. Ault's face. "I feel so bad for him. Every sound sets him off. He doesn't do it on purpose, Rose. But even though he's home he hasn't really left there. It's horrible. Even worse than his reaction is knowing that he saw so much. He tells us stories in pieces, but he can only go so far. Sometimes he thinks he's back there again and every noise . . . every little noise sends him spiraling."

Compassion compelled Rose. She hurried forward and wrapped her arms around the older woman's shoulders. She had never hugged her neighbor before. They'd always been kind to each other, but since they were *Englisch* and she was Amish there was a dividing line. Only now . . . Well, it just seemed right, necessary.

"I know you didn't mean it, Mrs. Ault, but we are so thankful for him, for his service. I've read the news reports. We had no idea what had really been happening with those camps, with the prisons, on the beaches . . ."

Rose's words cut short. It was the first time she'd spoken

such things out loud. It was a truth she hadn't thought about much. She'd been so concerned about the pain of Jonathan's betrayal that she hadn't really allowed thankfulness to sink in.

Thanksgiving.

She was thankful for the soldiers who served—and even thankful for Jonathan's part caring for men like Harold, though she'd never admitted it before, even to herself.

"It's so hard, Rose. Harold says things I don't understand. He does things . . ."

"But what did he mean?" Rose pulled back. "That part about me being rescued? What was it that you told him about me?"

"Oh, dear. He sometimes just says things." Mrs. Ault's words came too easily, gushing out. "He doesn't often know what he's—" She looked away and fiddled with the dish towel folded on the countertop.

"You don't know, then?" Rose said, peering into the woman's face. "You don't know why he would think that?"

Mrs. Ault bit her lip. "Like I just said, Harold says things and does things. Just last night . . . Oh, it was horrible. He was out there in the snow, huddled down behind a drift as if it was the sands of Iwo Jima. If it wasn't for that sweet Jonathan Fisher bringing him in—"

"Jonathan was here?" Rose's stomach flipped just hearing his name. *It was him.*

"Yes. His wagon was outside. It appeared he was delivering his last load of lumber."

"Seems out of his way to make a delivery," Rose commented more to herself than to Mrs. Ault.

"I don't know why he was doing what he was doing, dear. All I know is that the kind man humored Harold. He played along with him for a moment until Harold came to his senses again and came inside. That was the worst episode yet, and I hope it's the last. He's been home a week; surely he should be better soon. I'm just so thankful that kind Amish man knew how to help. And that he was there. An answer to my prayers, I tell you."

"He's seen things too." Rose's voice was soft. "I'm sure Jonathan's seen many men like Harold."

Tears filled Rose's eyes and a longing to see Jonathan overwhelmed her. Those feelings betrayed her. Jonathan had betrayed her. They'd talked of marriage and then he'd aligned himself with the world. He'd left her to face their community alone—a community that also felt betrayed.

Emotions crashed through her chest, pulling at her like waves on a battlefield shore. She was angry with him, yet she also worried about his anger when he discovered *her* truth. What would he say when he discovered her parents were *Englisch*? She was almost afraid to find out. But she had to talk to someone. Rose knew it would take swallowing her pride—her own feelings of betrayal—to allow that to happen.

But . . . she wasn't ready . . . not yet. Maybe she'd never be ready.

"Do you know if Jonathan's coming back . . . to see your son?" Rose asked.

"I'm not sure, dear. I really didn't ask him, but I hope he thinks of it. Maybe Harold will appreciate being with someone else who understands. He's asked about some of his other friends—some of his other schoolmates that he was especially fond of. I haven't the heart to tell him that two of his closest friends lost their lives, and the third is still serving in Europe somewhere with occupational forces." Mrs. Ault clucked her tongue and shook her head. "Can you imagine that we celebrated victory? We celebrated that the war was over. Little did we know that it would never be over. Not as long as our soldiers carry the memories."

"That is true, Mrs. Ault." Rose tried to be patient. She'd lived next to this woman for as long as she could remember and knew how to carry on a conversation with her. But what Rose really wanted to know about was what Harold had said.

She fixed her gaze again on the older woman's eyes. "What Harold said, that part of me being rescued . . ." She let her voice trail off, unable to ask directly if he meant being rescued by the Yoder family. Because that was another thing she hadn't thought about—a fresh horror. Not only did her family abandon her, not only was she not Amish, but if Harold knew—if that was what he was talking about—then others from the community had to know too.

Was she living like a fool, playing the part of an Amish woman and believing it, when everyone else knew the truth?

"I'm not sure, Rose." From the quiver in Mrs. Ault's voice Rose knew she was holding back. "I tell you I'm not certain what will come out of his mouth."

"Whatever it is, I bet there's a bit of truth to it, Mrs. Ault." Rose stood and motioned to her offerings. "Like I said before, there is an apple pie, Harold's favorite. I hope he enjoys it. And I hope that your family has a wonderful—*gut*—day, expressing to God your thankfulness for all the things He has provided."

As Rose walked home, she tried to offer prayers of her own thankfulness—for her family, her community, her life—yet the words sounded hollow to her ears. How could she be thankful for a life that was more imagined than real? And what would happen now? Could she really go along playing this part while knowing the truth?

A tear slid down her cheek. The first of what she assumed would be many on this day.

How would she be able to trust anything—anyone—again? Jonathan had lied when he'd left. Her mem had hidden the truth. And her family . . . She'd been just a little girl when they'd left her.

Trust me. The words came as a gentle whisper to her soul. A glimmer of warmth touched her heart, and she paused for a moment. Was the God of the universe really speaking to her heart and asking her to trust Him?

Rose prayed that she could.

Seven

Rose kicked at the snow as she continued forward toward home, stirring up white tuffs. "God, I want to be thankful, I really do." She crossed her arms over her chest, wondering what her real family was doing today. Did they still live in California? Were they gathering together? Had they felt the loss of her presence? Rose's heart ached thinking about it. But the ache lessened as she neared the house. Her younger siblings were in the middle of a snowball fight.

"Let's get Rose!" Martha called.

Within seconds a dozen snowballs pelted her direction. One hit her leg, another her shoulder. The rest of the snowballs fell painfully short. A smile curled from Rose's lips, and she bent over.

"I suppose you do not know, but when I was your age Marcus always chose me for his team in snowball fights!" Rose scooped up snow with her mittened hands and quickly packed a snowball. She let it drop to the ground and made three more. More snowballs flew her direction, and Rose scooped up her snowballs and stood. She threw two at Matthew, hitting him in the stomach, then two more at Elizabeth. She was about to bend over and scoop up more snow when she noticed someone off to the side. A man was there, hunched over and making snowballs for little Louisa. He handed them to her and cheered as she threw them, even though they didn't go more than a few feet.

The pounding of Rose's heart told her who it was before her mind registered his form: Jonathan. *What is he doing here? Lord, why today of all days?* She was still trying to figure out how to face all of her family, now that she knew the truth. And now this?

Rose stood. Her knees softened slightly as she moved toward Jonathan, despite the flurry of snowballs. She touched her *kapp*, checking that it was in place, and wished she could still the butterflies dancing in her stomach. She jutted out her chin, telling herself not to be weak—to remember the pain his leaving had caused.

"*Wie gehts!*" he called. *How are you?* As if it had been hours—not days—since they'd seen each other. His smile assaulted her. Didn't he remember her last words? Her declaration that she did not want to see him again?

Rose crossed her arms over her chest. What was he doing here? Why had he come now? She didn't want to talk to him.

Well, she did, and that was the problem. Unlike anyone else, Jonathan had lived among the *Englisch*—had been a part of them. Maybe he could answer the questions about why her parents did what they did.

"Rose." He moved toward her, his face growing serious. It was only as he paused before her that he released the breath he'd been holding. "I'm sorry if I startled you. I know what you told me, but . . . I just can't sit by. More than that—my sister showed up at my house last night. She told me I was a fool if I gave up on you too easily. And my mother made some silly excuse that I needed to return one of your mem's serving dishes. I knew I wouldn't be able to pull up my chair to her table until I did. But since I'm here, I . . . I thought I'd tell you again how sorry I am."

"Stop." Rose raised her hand.

He rushed on. "Do you know, Rose, that I am truly sorry? I never meant to bring you shame—"

"Jonathan. Just stop." She pressed her hand to the front of his jacket, where snow clung in clumps from the impact of snowballs.

"You're not going to let me talk?" He raised one eyebrow.

"*Ne.*" She lowered her gaze, looking to his lips—lips that had kissed her forehead a dozen times. "I'm not going to let you . . . apologize. We can talk." She glanced up at him, keeping her voice firm. "I have more questions than answers, but we can talk."

"From the pinched look on yer face, Rose, they must be thorny questions." He chuckled, but seeing no humor in her face, swallowed once. His Adam's apple made a slow rise and fall. "All right. *Ja*, I imagine you want to know if I'm committed to being here, to staying Amish. Or maybe, like the others, you believe this community will no longer be able to hold me."

A headache formed in her left temple. "My thoughts

aren't on the future . . . not yet. I just got back from seeing Harold. Does the *Englisch* world always cause such pain, Jonathan?"

A haunted look came into Jonathan's eyes. "I don't know what I could tell you." He cleared his throat. "It's hard for me to talk about all I faced in the war. There are things you don't want to hear."

Rose believed his words, and she knew she couldn't force him. "I understand. Today is not the right time to discuss such things. Maybe not for a while."

"Not for a while . . . ," he echoed.

Rose brushed the snow off her mittens. Confusion built walls of defense inside her. He'd seemed so open in his letters. Maybe it was easier to write the pain than express it in words? Or maybe he was afraid she'd turn him away, like she had last week. If you kicked a puppy away enough times, it would eventually stop coming to you. Is that what she'd done to him? Her chest ached, realizing she had.

The children continued to play in the snow, and Jonathan turned his attention to their antics.

At least he was here. At least he'd tried again and had come to see her. It helped her anger subside some. She also appreciated that his sister and mem wanted him to come. Should she allow a bit of their hope to filter into her heart? Maybe she should. It would be a shame—for his family's sake—to turn him away too quickly.

Rose rubbed her stomach. "*Hungerich?*"

"*Ja*, a little."

"Will you stay . . . for the meal?" Rose's voice rose.

"I'm not sure." Relief came over his face, as if he was thankful she hadn't again brought up his leaving the Amish community.

"What do you mean?"

"Am I invited?" He cocked one eyebrow.

"I'm sure it'll be fine. I mean, of course it will be fine. My parents . . . uh . . . they've always liked you." She smiled. It was the most she could offer at the moment.

"*Gut*, because my sister told me not to come home until you and I had a chance to talk."

"She said that?"

He nodded and waved a hand. "Got tired of me moping around the house, she did."

"And tired of you driving by?"

His dark eyes widened. "You know?"

"My little sister squealed. Mrs. Ault told me too. I . . . was there just now."

Reading the unspoken thoughts on her face, Jonathan sighed. "I feel so bad for her . . . for Harold."

"I'm just starting to understand, starting to realize, how bad it must have been. And the sacrifice." A shiver ran down her spine. "I thought for so long that there was a right way and a wrong way. I thought . . ." She stopped. How could she explain that although, according to the bishop, she'd been the one in the right, it did not matter now. Her good living and good choices couldn't change who she really was. Her works couldn't make up for her heritage.

The sun above seemed to fade a little. *What will Jonathan do when he knows the truth?*

Jonathan looked back at the house. "We need to get inside. You look like you're getting a chill."

"*Ja*, of course." Rose led the way to the house, her heart torn. A warm kitchen, a happy family, Jonathan by her side—nothing could change what was at her core, how she felt.

Abandoned. Lost. Afraid.

She had everything—more than everything—right here in this home, but it didn't belong to her. Not really.

Trust Me. The stirring came from within again.

"I wish I could." The words were less than a whisper. "I wish I could." She reached her hand for the door.

"Listen." Jonathan's voice from behind startled her. Rose paused and turned. "I know I told you the same thing last week, but I want you to be assured. Rose, I won't be walking in the way of the world. I saw a lot, but . . . but I like what this world—our world—has to offer better."

She'd heard those words, but most in the community doubted them. She doubted them.

She also doubted that either of them would be fully welcomed into this community when the others found out the truth of who she really was.

"I want to believe you, I really do, but you didn't tell the truth when you left, did you?" Rose lowered her voice. "Besides, what if it never works? What if the community doesn't forget? What if leaving the Amish is the best answer after all?"

Eight

THERE WASN'T A FREE PLACE TO SIT IN THE YODERS' house. After a quiet morning of fasting and contemplation, Rose's stomach rumbled as she mashed potatoes for their Thanksgiving meal. A group of children watched her—their eyes wide, hungry. Jonathan watched her too. Questions, so many questions, filled his gaze.

She checked the green beans simmering in a large pot, a gust of steam rising as she lifted the lid.

In addition to her siblings, her aunt Bertha and uncle Eli were there with their nine children, and their oldest daughter, Rebekah, with her husband and new *boppli*. Vera and LeRoy had slipped in right before it was time to serve the food. Little Ira had a tummy ache, and they'd had a rough morning.

Rose's aunt and uncle and cousins seemed uncomfortable to see Jonathan there. There had been so much talk about him around the community that it almost seemed they'd forgotten he was a real person—and someone Rose cared about.

Once they were all seated, Dat spoke. "Before we eat,

let's all share one thing we are thankful for." He looked around. "*Aenti* Bertha, since it's your birthday, why don't you start?"

"I'm thankful for our ancestors who stood up to persecution so we could know the truth. They died so we could live for our Lord." Tears filled the corners of her eyes and her voice quivered.

"I'm thankful for a good harvest this year," Uncle Eli spoke next. "The barns are full. The shelves are too."

They continued around the room, her cousins and siblings thankful for health, for family, and for their community.

"Mary, what about you?" Dat turned to Mem.

She folded her hands on her lap. "I'm thankful for the children God granted me to raise . . . all eight of them. They are a gift to me, each and every one. I don't love one more than any other. I carry them close to my heart." Her voice trembled as she spoke, and the house grew quiet. She wiped a tear and then glanced up, looking at Rose.

"Rose, I believe yer the last one." Dat's gaze was intense, and she was certain Mem had told him about their conversation—and how she knew the truth.

"*Ne*. I'm not the only one left." Rose glanced over to Jonathan, who sat beside her. "Jonathan still has to go yet."

"You first, Rose." He nodded his chin in her direction.

Rose glanced from Jonathan to Dat to Mem. "I'm—I—" She blew out a soft breath. "I'm thankful that my Lord knows me better than even I know myself. I'm thankful He watches over me, even on the coldest nights."

There were a few nods in the room, but puzzled looks from the younger ones. She breathed a little easier because of that. They didn't understand—not yet—but she knew that someday, most likely soon, the truth would be known to all.

"I am thankful too." Jonathan leaned forward slightly in his seat. "That because of our Lord, good wins over evil. Because of our Lord we can have hope in this life." He glanced at Rose. "With God we can always cling to hope."

DINNER HAD BEEN EATEN IN ONE QUARTER OF THE TIME it took to make it. Telling her that he had to get back to visit with family, Jonathan left with a promise that they'd talk sometime in the next few days. After the meal, the rest of the family—except for Rose, Vera, and baby Ira—left to travel just a mile down the road to visit with Mem's youngest sister, who'd given birth to a baby girl two weeks ago.

Rose stoked the fire. Vera's hands were up to her elbows in dishwater when baby Ira began to cry from the cradle. "Would you mind holding him?" Vera asked. "He's getting hungry, but I just need five more minutes."

"*Ja*, of course." Rose put down the poker and hurried over to the cradle that rocked ever so slightly with the flailing of Ira's small arms. "There, now."

Ira's cries softened at her voice. She wrapped the blanket tighter around him and scooped him up. His cry turned into a whimper, and she moved to the rocking chair. She tucked him in the crook of one arm and leaned down so her nose nearly touched his. His blond eyebrows were a feathery arch. Rose nuzzled her nose against his cheek, and he grunted, opened his mouth, and turned.

"He's hungry, all right." She chuckled, sticking the tip of her finger into his mouth. He sucked vigorously.

Vera finished the last of the dishes, setting the final tin cup on a white dish towel to dry. Then she wiped her hands.

"Don't worry about the water. I'll dump it. Come feed your son." Rose lifted from the chair and handed the baby over. Vera settled down and within a minute the baby was contentedly nursing. Vera looked over at Rose with questions in her eyes. Did Vera wonder why Jonathan was here today—what had changed?

"Jest think." Vera ran her finger down Ira's cheek. "Maybe before long you'll have one of these."

Rose pressed her fists into her hips. "Vell, Jonathan and I need time to talk. I was angry with him when he returned from the war, and I'm only slightly less angry now. This is only the second time I've seen him since he's been back. I'm not sure what he thinks about things—about me." Rose studied her sister, gauging her response, wondering if she had the guts to ask her outright if she knew the truth.

Vera shook her head. "Oh, Rose. How could you say that? Did you not see the way he looked at you? He was so spit shined today I could see my reflection in his cheeks!"

Rose moved to Mem's rocker and pulled white thread and a needle from the basket on the floor. Like Mem, she always had to be doing something. One opened oneself to the devil's work when hands grew idle—or at least that's what Mem had always said.

"I'd say he has a wedding on his mind," Vera continued. "And I'd tell you that, by the look in his eye, he doesn't want to wait until next fall. Of course nobody asked me," she added with a wink.

Rose had noticed the difference too. Jonathan had always been more comfortable in the fields, tending to his dat's dairy cows. As a boy, he was teased for the stench he often carried in on his boots—if he wore any. A grade older than him, Rose hadn't thought much of Jonathan then, but when she approached her seventeenth year, Jonathan made his interest clear.

Now he'd seen the world. He'd cared for soldiers. He'd used his skill to tend the wounded. And even though there was uncertainty in his gaze concerning her, Jonathan walked with sure steps. She couldn't call it pride—Jonathan was anything but prideful. But she could tell by his walk he'd done a great work. She could also see pain in his gaze. Was there something else too? True love for her? Not the giddy love they'd felt before he left, but the solid love that could overcome trials?

"So, Rose . . ." Vera's words interrupted her thoughts. "I have to know: what changed things? I was surprised to see Jonathan here today. Last time we spoke you were disappointed in him. You didn't want to talk to him, after what he'd done."

Rose set her tatting to the side. "Mem didn't tell you?"

"*Ne*. Tell me what?"

"I know the truth, Vera. I realize I should not be so harsh on Jonathan when I . . ."

Vera paused her rocking slightly. "The truth about what?" The gaiety had disappeared from her eyes, replaced by a troubled frown.

Rose straightened in her seat. The grim reality that they weren't really sisters settled as an ache in her chest. She felt a stab of remorse for bringing it up now. *I should have just enjoyed this moment with Vera . . . enjoyed the talk of Jonathan's love.*

"Rose?" Vera's voice raised an octave. She placed the baby on her shoulder to burp him.

"The truth of who I am. The truth of my real parents."

Vera's mouth opened slightly. "You didn't know?"

"No . . . I didn't. How could I know that?" Rose felt her lips draw into a taut line. "And you knew this whole time and didn't say something. Maybe it could have come up in a conversation once or twice: *'Rose, do ya ever wonder why we don't look alike? Why you look not like anyone else in our family.'* Maybe you could have told me a little about the people who birthed me. That would have been a start."

"Surely you remember them, Rose."

"Barely. Just a few memories, but for so long I thought they were just part of a dream."

"A dream?" Vera bounced the baby as she patted his back. "I just assumed you'd remember."

"Didn't you wonder why I never talked about them?"

"I just thought it was too hard." Vera's lower lip quivered. "*Ne*. It was more than that. I believed that you didn't need to talk about them—that you became part of *our* family. I thought that we were all you needed . . . You fit in so well. You have to admit, Rose, that you have a special bond with both Dat and Mem. There were times I daresay I was even jealous. The rest of us came from Mem, but you were an unexpected gift."

"You're jest saying all this, trying to make me feel better."

"Is that what you think?"

"I don't know what I think anymore." An ache grew in Rose's heart. "I don't know how I feel, except for the sense I don't fit in—not anywhere."

They both sat quietly for a moment, the ticking of the clock and the rocking of their chairs on the wooden floor the only sounds. Vera's face grew ashen, and she looked at the fireplace with a vacant stare. Rose's words hadn't been kind, but they were the truth. If this family loved her, surely they should have said something more—could have done something more to help her understand before now.

"When did Mem tell you about your family and whatnot?"

"Last night."

"Did you feel as if you fit in yesterday?"

"*Ja*."

"Then . . . remember that, Rose. When the *ferhoodled* thoughts come, remember you do have a place. You are with us for a reason. Your heart was settled here, was it not? Knowing about *them* doesn't change anything about *us*."

They sat quietly after that. Rose wanted to believe Vera's words, but nothing seemed further than the truth. She'd fit in before because she didn't know any different. But now?

Rose peered out the window, wondering if it was the clomping of horse's hooves she heard coming down the road or the creaking of the breeze in the trees. After a minute she knew it was only the breeze.

She thought again about the letter left by her birth mother for Mem and Dat. She thought too about the package Stan and Betty had left. What had been in it?

She looked at the wind-up clock on the wall, shocked by how many hours had passed since her family had left. She stood and moved to the window. It was dark out there; night had draped over them, but had provided no warmth in doing so.

"Don't worry. I'm sure they jest got a late start," Vera said. "You know how Dat gets when he and Ruth's Samuel get talking about their childhood hunting trips."

Rose nodded, but the knots in her stomach didn't loosen. Maybe that was the reason for the mounting tension—she hated for the house to be so quiet. She didn't like her family gone and the rooms so hollow. With so many brothers and sisters there was rarely a quiet moment, but the quiet—the stillness—caused her more pain than any storm.

If I left it would mean quiet rooms . . . Then I'd truly be alone. The thought was more than she could bear. How could she leave the Amish, leave her family? Even if it meant she would never know about her real family, she wouldn't be alone. The unknowing would be easier than the leaving, the missing, wouldn't it?

Outside the wind picked up, and something banged around on the porch. She was certain she heard the buggy now. Rose hurried to the window and then slipped into her sweater, rushing outside. The icy air smacked her forehead and seeped through her layered clothing. She tucked the sweater tighter around herself, to no avail.

The black buggy matched the night, but she could make out the motion of the wheel spokes turning until the buggy stopped just outside the barn.

"Rose, yer going to catch the fright of cold." Mem was the first down off the buggy. "Is everything all right? Anything wrong with Vera? With the *boppli?*"

"*Ne*, everything's fine. I was just seeing if you needed help with anything." Rose grasped her mem's hands in her own. She clung to Mem's wool mittens as if they were a lifeline.

Mem frowned and concern flashed in her gaze. "I'm here now." She helped Louisa off the buggy, then turned back and weaved her arm through Rose's. They walked together toward the house.

"Is anything the matter?" Mem asked again.

"There are things you haven't told me yet–like what was inside the package. Mem, I need to know everything."

Nine

THEY WAITED UNTIL HER OLDER SIBLINGS AND FAMILIES had left. They waited until the little ones were put to bed. They waited until Dat left them with a soft "G'night" as he headed upstairs.

Rose pulled out one of the kitchen chairs and stood as she watched Mem sink down into the one across from her. Dat had built the long table when they were first married. He'd had so much faith they'd have a large family together, he'd used long planks without cutting them down.

"Tea?" Rose asked.

"*Ne*. Thank ye, though." The look on Mem's face made it clear this was not a sociable visit. The same ache as the time she'd lost a baby after the twins were born pulled heavy on her face.

Her mother looked weary. So weary.

"Mem, can you tell me what happened next?" It was one question. The one Rose had been thinking about again and again. She sat, running her hand over the smooth wood of the table that had hosted hundreds of meals in this growing family.

"They were gone." Mem smoothed her apron. "No one saw them go, of course. No one was looking or watching. Why would they?"

Rose sat silent, waiting for her mem to continue.

"We asked around town, and we kept asking. The first night everything was fine. It was as if you were just sleeping over. We had potato soup, and you ate more than Dat that night. We started realizing then how bad off things had been."

"And after the first night?"

Mem's lower lip quivered. "It was so hard to hear you cry. You wanted your mom, your dad, and your older brothers. And you asked about your little sister the most. You'd shared a bed with her, we finally figured out. I think you felt responsible for Daisy. You didn't understand that she had died. Everyone was gone and you couldn't understand why."

"Daisy?"

"*Ja*, Rose. That was her name. Yer mother did enjoy flowers."

"It makes sense, then." Rose didn't ask about her brothers. How many older brothers did she have? Sometimes faces had come to her in her dreams, smiling blond boys, but it was enough just to think of her little sister for a while.

"How long was I sad, Mem?"

"Things got better when you started sharing a bed with Vera. And . . ." Mem looked away. "At first we tried to keep your family's memory alive, but ev'ry time we brought them up it just brought pain. Soon it was easier jest to stop talking about them completely. I don't know if it was the right thing. I don't know . . ."

Rose stood and moved toward her mother. She sank onto the floor next to her. How many days had she sat by her mother's feet as a child—just so she could be close to her and watch her mend or sew? More than she could count.

Rose knew she should focus on all that was good in her life. That's what this day—Thanksgiving—was about. God had cared for her and brought her into this family. She had grown and become strong and healthy in so many ways.

"In a year's time you fit right in and stopped asking about your family," Mem said. "We also moved the five miles from Charm to Berlin to be closer to my parents. They both passed away the next year, but we stayed. There were many times I wanted to talk to you about it, Rose, but the truth was I forgot in a way too. You seemed mine." Mem reached out and patted Rose's head. "You are mine . . . and don't you forget it."

Rose didn't say anything. She just stared at Mem's simple black shoes, wondering about her younger sister. *Daisy*. She couldn't picture her face, but she guessed she'd had blonde hair too.

"Jonathan . . . Does he know?" Mem's voice interrupted Rose's thoughts.

"*Ne*. I've yet to tell him."

"I'm sure he'll understand," Mem said. "He of all people."

Rose knew what Mem meant, and she sank back a little. Jonathan might be able to understand, but would the community? She'd heard what they said when he'd chosen to help as a medic. She'd seen how they treated that *Englischer* who'd tried to become Amish. They hadn't confronted her. They didn't act out against her. Instead they showed only the minimum of kindness that made it clear she was not one of them. What would they say when they discovered the truth about her?

Unless some already knew. Rose's brow furrowed as she considered Harold's words today. He'd thought of her while he was fighting. Thought of her rescue. She pushed out a heavy breath. No, she couldn't think about that now.

"The package, Rose." Mem lifted her gaze. "Do you want me to get it?"

Rose shook her head. There was enough filling her mind to rob her of any hope of sleep as it was. Enough to weigh on her heart. Rose released a sigh. "Not tonight. I think I'll try to rest." Rose stood and let her hand linger on Mem's arm. "I told Lucy I'd help at the school tomorrow."

"It's good of you to be there for your friend." Mem rose, too, an inch at a time, as if she didn't have enough energy to do it all at once.

Rose hoped she could get some sleep. Sleep would keep the questions at bay . . . unless the dreams, the nightmares, came again. Last night she'd fallen asleep, and instead of searching the same small house—as she'd always done in her dream—she'd walked down a long, endless road.

What had she been looking for?

As she walked to her room, she thought about the Bible story Dat used to read to her and her siblings as a child. It was one that Jesus told about a man who'd had ninety-nine sheep but lost one. She'd never really thought about herself as the lost sheep, until now. Did her birth mother and father still think of her? Maybe so, but they'd never come back. They'd left without looking back. They hadn't tried to find her over the years.

Once in her room, she sat on her bed and pictured the shepherd finding the sheep, putting it on his shoulders, and carrying it back to celebrate. She'd been found. She should be thankful. But as Rose drifted off to a fitful sleep ten minutes later, she pictured the sheep still bleating with mournful cries. Even though the fold she was taken to was wonderful, it wasn't her fold . . . the one where she belonged.

DAWN HAD BARELY REACHED ACROSS THE WHOLE expanse of sky when Rose walked the mile to the clapboard one-room schoolhouse. Even though it was only 8:40 a.m., she was late and the door was shut tight. The one window was also shut tight, boarded up for winter to keep out the cold. To anyone passing by it would be hard to believe the small box was filled with a dozen children, but Rose knew that within a few minutes time she'd be surrounded with noise and lantern light and life.

Her best friend growing up—called Miss Lucy now—had always played school with her younger siblings. She'd been a natural choice to teach and had done so since she was sixteen. Of course, the way Rose had seen her and Benjamin Müller spending time together, she guessed it would be the last year Lucy taught. Rose had no doubt by next fall Lucy would be a bride. Something she wished she could say about herself. Something she felt robbed of . . . by decisions not her own.

Rose mounted the steps to the school. Tucked inside her coat was a copy of *Heidi*. It had been her and Lucy's favorite book growing up, and they had often read it, and other books, to each other by candlelight during sleepovers. Even Vera—who didn't care much for reading—would sit and listen while they took turns reading back and forth. And ever since Lucy had started teaching, that had been Rose's job—coming to school once a week to read a chapter to the students. She enjoyed it as much as they did.

She opened the door to the classroom, and heat from the potbelly stove hit her face.

"Hurray!" An excited cheer rose up from some of the girls. Even the boys did not seem disappointed. One child near the front—also named Louisa—raised her hand as soon as she saw Rose.

Lucy stood in the front of the room. She was petite and could be mistaken for one of the students by anyone who didn't know better. Lucy chuckled. "*Ja*, Louisa, you can go and get Miss Rose's coat."

Louisa had made it her chore every week to retrieve Rose's simple blue wool coat and hang it on the hook closest to the fire so that it would be warm for Rose when she prepared to walk home.

"Miss Rose!" Louisa exclaimed, approaching her. "Will

Heidi be able to return to her grandfather today?" This was Louisa's second year in school, and she had already heard the story last year, although none of the students seemed to mind hearing it again.

Rose slipped her arms out of her jacket, and then tucked her gloves into one inside pocket before handing the coat over to her small helper. "I'm not certain, Louisa." She winked. "We'll just have to see, won't we?"

Louisa scampered toward the front of the room where the potbelly stove stood, and Rose noticed many eyes turned toward her. Others were setting aside their books and papers, readying themselves to hear the story.

Rose took two steps and then paused. Emotion overwhelmed her as she noticed the sea of girls in *kapps* and boys in Amish haircuts. She'd sat in this very room for all her studies, and she'd imagined her children doing the same. But was that possible now? What would the bishop say? Would he allow such a thing as her marrying an Amishman?

"Rose, are you feeling all right?" It was Lucy's voice breaking through the fog of her mind.

Rose glanced up and noticed all eyes on her. "Oh, *ja*." She rubbed her hands together. "I'm still jest a little chilled, but I'm *gut*."

She hurried forward to the chair Lucy had set up for her. As Rose prepared to sit, Lucy caught her arm. "If you're under the weather, Rose . . ."

"*Ne*." As hard as she tried, she couldn't blink away a thin layer of tears fast enough. "I am *gut*. It's just . . ."

Lucy leaned in to whisper in Rose's ear. "Jonathan?"

Rose nodded slightly. That was only part of it, but she knew now wasn't the time to explain the rest. Or ever. Could she always hide the truth? She could try, but it would be an unbearable burden to carry. Better to let it out and then deal with the consequences.

Rose sat on a wooden stool in the front of the class and opened the book to chapter eleven.

"Heidi Gains in One Way and Loses in Another," Rose read aloud in a strong, clear voice. Deep inside she wished it was the same for her. As far as she was concerned, there was no gain in what she faced.

The chapter started with Clara's grandmother showing Heidi her pretty dolls and how to make dresses and pinafores for them, so that Heidi learned to sew. Grandmother also enjoyed Heidi's reading, but something was missing for Heidi. Someone.

"She entered into the lives of all the people she read about so that they became like dear friends to her, and it delighted her more and more to be with them," Rose read. "But still Heidi never looked really happy, and her bright eyes were no longer to be seen. It was the last week of Grandmother's visit. She called Heidi to her room as usual one day after dinner, and the child came with her book under her arm. The grandmother called her to come close, and then laying the book aside, said, 'Now, child, tell me why you are not happy? Have you still the same trouble at heart?'"

The room was silent as Rose read. Every eye was fixed

on her and the only sound was the soft breaths of children and the occasional shuffling on one of the long benches as two boys settled in. Lucy's eyes bore into her, and Rose dared to glance over at her young friend between sentences. Lucy's worried eyes asked the same question Grandmother had just asked Heidi: "*Have you still the same trouble at heart?*"

"Heidi nodded in reply," Rose read on, her eyes fixed on the page.

"'Have you told God about it?'"

"'Yes.'"

"'And do you pray every day that He will make things right and that you may be happy again?'"

"'No, I have left off praying.'"

"'Do not tell me that, Heidi! Why have you left off praying?'"

"'It is of no use, God does not listen,' Heidi went on in an agitated voice, 'and I can understand that when there are so many, many people in Frankfurt praying to Him every evening that He cannot attend to them all, and He certainly had not heard what I said to Him.'"

"'And why are you so sure of that, Heidi?'"

"'Because I have prayed for the same thing every day for weeks, and yet God has not done what I asked.'"

"'You are wrong, Heidi; you must not think of Him like that. God is a good father to us all, and knows better than we do what is good for us. If we ask Him for something that is not good for us, He does not give it, but something better still, if only we will continue to pray earnestly and do not run away and lose our trust in Him. God did not think what you have been praying for was good for you just now, but be sure He heard you, for He can hear and see everyone at the same time, because He is a God and not a human being like you and me. And because He thought it was better for you not to have at once what you wanted, He said to Himself: Yes, Heidi shall have what she asks for, but not until the right time comes, so that she may be quite happy. If I do what she wants now, and then one day she sees that it would have been better for her not to have had her own way, she will cry and say, "If only God had not given me what I asked for! It is not so good as I expected!" And while God is watching over you, and looking to see if you will trust Him and go on praying to Him every day, and turn to Him for everything you want, you run away and leave off saying your prayers, and forget all about Him . . .'"

Rose continued on, and the children listened intently. Finally, after another ten minutes of reading, she closed the book and considered poor Heidi in a way she never had before.

How many times had Rose read this same passage? Dozens. But it had never pained her heart as it did now. The words pierced her, as if each letter was a small knife. She'd always agreed with Grandmother before. She had always inwardly cheered at her monologue. But this time Rose was pained at Grandmother for not understanding.

It was a hard chapter to read, and more than once she'd had to pause and wipe away a stray tear. Her sister Louisa, on the front bench, looked concerned. The other Louisa had started to cry softly over Heidi's terrible homesickness. Seeing the young girl's tears, Rosa's throat grew thick and tight.

Rose stayed for another hour, helping Lucy by listening to the younger ones read, but when it was time for Rose to head home, it felt as if all her energy had been drained from her. Her arms felt like thick, heavy logs as she pushed them through her coat sleeves.

As she'd read about Heidi's longing for the world in the mountains—beyond the white walls of Clara's fine house—Rose had understood that feeling, of missing what had been there for so long. It was homesickness. Even when her mind didn't remember, her heart knew.

Heidi lived within a luxurious home and had more fine things than she could imagine. Heidi had a good friend in Clara. Clara's family had taken her in as their own. And still she ached for what was lost.

And Rose's losses seemed to be multiplying.

She'd been so hard on Jonathan, but had she really taken the time to think about what she was giving up? She'd been so focused on how the community felt, but had she really allowed herself to think how she felt about Jonathan . . . and how he would feel when she turned her back?

Why hadn't she been more open—to Jonathan and to God?

Rose slipped on her mittens, preparing to leave, thinking of Grandmother's words. "*God knows better. He knows the right time to answer your prayers.*" It made sense that perhaps the time wasn't right for her and Jonathan, but what couldn't be right about living with one's birth family? Had her mom prayed for a different way? She hoped so. Not that the prayer was answered.

Was it true that someday she'd thank God for those unanswered prayers too?

Ten

BUNDLED UP, ROSE BID THE CHILDREN GOOD-BYE AND prepared for the mile-long walk home. The cold wind—which carried tiny ice crystals from a soft flurry of snow—hit her cheeks as she walked outside. There, sitting in front of the school, was a wagon. Rose stopped short. The back was filled with long planks of lumber, and Jonathan was perched on the front bench.

"Need a ride?" he called.

Rose crossed her arms over her chest. Part of her was happy to see him. But part of her feared again growing close to Jonathan. Feared having to tell him her truth. Yet, as she gazed at his bright eyes and wide smile, Rose couldn't help smiling back. "How did you know? What are you doing here?"

"Don't you always read to the children on Fridays?"

"*Ja.*" Rose didn't ask how he knew that.

"Then would you like a ride?"

She nodded and moved down the stairs, hurrying across the schoolyard with quickened steps. "But it's only a mile."

"A mile you don't have to walk now." He reached a hand down toward her as she lifted her foot to climb aboard.

Rose hoisted herself up into the wagon, and Jonathan scooted over. "Here . . . I'll even let you have my warm spot."

She sat without argument, the words of Heidi's grandmother coming to her once again. Perhaps she did understand a bit more about them than she'd thought. By wishing she'd stayed with her birth family, she was negating all she'd experienced and felt with those she'd grown up with. She would have missed out on Dat, Mem, and her siblings. She wouldn't be sitting here now, with Jonathan.

"Hey-ya," Jonathan called to his horse. The wagon wheels squeaked on the snow, accompanied by the sounds of rocks being crunched as they left the schoolyard.

They shared small talk. He discussed his work. "I'd much rather be working on the farm, but delivering lumber in the winter helps Dat and Mem."

She talked about reading to the children and about Heidi's homesickness. "Sometimes you don't realize what you have until you lose it—not that losing it was Heidi's choice," she rattled on as if Jonathan understood what she was talking about.

"Would *you* ever consider leaving the area, Rose?" Jonathan asked.

"Not before."

"Before?" The way he said it, it was obvious he thought she meant before he left for the war. Jonathan had no idea she meant before three days ago.

Rose shrugged. "Why are you asking?"

"The other day, before we were interrupted, you said you

wanted to talk to me. You mentioned you'd thought about leaving."

"I've thought about it, but not seriously." How could she tell him the truth? "Don't most people think about it?"

"Not most people, Rose. Most people are content to walk in the way of their ancestors. To choose the Amish life and believe it's the only . . . *right* . . . way." The way he dragged out the last few words, it was as if he was asking her a question. Was that what she believed too?

They neared her house, but instead of slowing the horse continued on. Rose forced a chuckle to ease the tension between them. "Did you forget something?"

"I thought we'd have some lunch in town . . . if you don't mind." Jonathan lowered his head slightly. She studied the tufts of dark hair that covered the tops of his ears. Her heartbeat jumped into her throat.

To sit across from him. To look into his eyes. She wondered how long she'd be able to keep her secret. Yet even as she thought of telling him her throat cinched.

"Vell . . ." She tried to come up with a good excuse, but there was none. Mem was at a quilting circle, her siblings were at school, and there was nothing—no one—who needed her.

"If you'd rather not, I understand. "He pointed behind his shoulder. "I can turn around. I understand what people are saying about me—about my choice. I know that I've lost the approval of many in our community. I've lost your approval." He sighed heavily. "I'm afraid I've lost yer heart too."

"There is so much more you don't understand, Jonathan.

It's not easy to explain how I'm feeling . . . what I'm thinking. Some days I can't figure it out myself."

The snow-covered fields of Holmes County rose and fell, stretching out on either side of the road. Here or there an oblique lump or mound marred the landscape. Rose knew if she got out and brushed the snow off she'd find familiar tree stumps or piles of fencing. In a way, that's how her emotions felt—she knew more was beneath, but it took too much effort to brush away the protective layer she'd built around her heart.

"Will you *try* to tell me, Rose?"

"I'm sorry, Jonathan. I should have taken more time to listen to you when you returned. I should have read your letters with an open heart, instead of being so worried about what the bishop thought, what others thought."

He looked over at her. His eyes widened slightly as she studied his face. "Do you mean that?"

"*Ja*," she said, realizing she did mean it.

"I'm ready to listen when you tell me, Rose." He leaned forward slightly and his lips parted. For a moment she thought he was going to kiss her.

Rose pulled her head back, knowing he wouldn't want to do that. Not if he knew.

The disappointment was clear on Jonathan's face.

"Do you mind if I drop this lumber off first?"

"*Ne*, don't mind. Not at all."

The buggy stopped at Hummel's Grocery. The building was on Main Street, and large glass windows displayed full shelves. It seemed strange being able to see inside the store. During the war, the windows had been covered with war bond posters. Rose believed Mr. Hummel was patriotic, but she also guessed that the posters had hidden the limited supply of items on the store shelves.

"Why don't you head inside and keep warm? I'm going to take this lumber 'round back. They need it in the back storeroom to build some new shelves."

"*Ja*, of course."

Inside the glass front door, warm air and the scent of baking bread greeted her. One of the clerks was checking out a customer at the front counter. He turned in her direction.

"Why, hello there." His fingers paused from entering prices into the register before he went back to checking out the customer. But instead of talking to the older *Englisch* woman at the counter, he glanced again at Rose. "I've seen you in here before, with your mem. She seems like a nice lady."

He didn't look familiar, but obviously he knew her, so she had to have met him before. He hadn't lived long in Berlin, though; she was certain of that. "*Ja*, she is. I—I am blessed to have my family."

He nodded and went back to punching the keys as vigorously as before.

She glanced around, trying to figure out how to spend her time. She didn't have a shopping list and not a penny with her. She hadn't planned on going anywhere but the school. Yet she walked down the canned goods aisle with purpose.

It was nice to see the shelves full again. Rationing during

the war had been hard for many. More than once they'd had neighbors stop by to ask her parents if they had any extra eggs or meat to sell. Her parents always seemed to find something to offer, even if it meant they ate vegetable soup for dinner.

She moved to the far corner of the store where the meat counter was, pretending that the sign that read the prices of the meat was as interesting as her story from *Heidi*.

"Pot Roast of Beef, 29 cents a pound. Fresh ground hamburger, 28 cents a pound. Breakfast sausages, small link, 44 cents," she said to no one in particular.

The butcher approached from the back room wearing a red-and-white-striped shirt, a white apron that looked as if it had just been pulled off the clothes line, and a straw hat. He was an imposing man in girth and stature, but he wore a nice smile. "Can I help you, miss?"

"Oh, no, Mr. Milligan," she said. "I'm just looking today . . . and waiting for a friend."

"Ah, yes. Jonathan is unloading the wood for the new shelves in back. We're blessed to have run out of room for stock. We have quite the construction project going on back there."

"I think everyone feels blessed." Rose offered a smile. "It's *gut* to have all our boys coming home."

"I imagine especially that one." Mr. Milligan pointed his thumb over his shoulder toward the back supply room. "Don't think the people in the community don't understand the sacrifice. And as someone who had a son come home in one piece, I thank Jonathan every time I see him."

Rose nodded but didn't know how to respond. Just as she was figuring out what to say, she heard the shuffling of footsteps behind her. She turned to see the cashier approaching. He leaned on a cane and walked with a limp.

Rose's heart fell, and she understood now why she didn't remember seeing him around before. He was a returning soldier who'd somehow landed in Berlin.

The cashier used his cane to point to his left kneecap. "It was a bullet. And the Jap was either a great shot and just wanted to slow me down, or he missed by a long shot when aiming for my heart."

Rose offered a sympathetic smile. "Iwo Jima?"

The man shook his head. "No, I missed that one, but Saipan was no tea party." He limped over to the cold case next to the meat counter and pulled out two Coca-Colas. Gripping them both in his left hand, he reached into his pocket with his right hand and pulled out a bottle opener. He popped both lids, dropped the bottle opener back into his apron pocket, and offered her a drink.

"Oh, no, I couldn't." She held up her palm, refusing his offer.

"Have you ever had a cola before?" The light-haired man tilted his head to the side and studied her in a way that made her want to escape out into the cold.

"*Ne*. I mean, no." She shook her head vigorously. "But—" What excuse did she have? Any excuse. She lightly touched the top of her white head covering.

"Of course!" The man set one of the colas on the meat

counter and extended his hand to her. "I should have introduced myself. I'm Curtis. Curtis Williams." His gaze drifted up to the head covering she wore from morning to night.

"Nice to meet you, Curtis." She looked back to the butcher, hoping to pull him into the conversation, but he'd slipped into the back room.

Not knowing what else to do, Rose extended her hand and shook Curtis's, and then forced a smile as she accepted the cola.

"Go ahead. Take a sip. It's on me."

Rose lifted the bottle to her lips and opened her mouth.

Curtis laughed. "You don't pour it into your mouth. You press it to your lips, like this." Curtis turned his head and showed her how. Rose shrugged and then attempted it.

The liquid was so cold that it stung her teeth. There was a bubbly feeling to it and the sweetness caused her to wince and blink her eyes rapidly. She pulled the bottle away from her mouth and the liquid splashed onto her chin. Laughter burst from Curtis, and he covered his mouth with the back of his hand.

"Well," he sputtered between breaths. "Do you like it?"

Rose shrugged again. "Not really . . . although I'm sorry if that offends you."

"Offends me? No." He took the bottle from her and placed it on top of the glass meat counter. "There are few things in this life that offend me. In fact—"

Footsteps sounded from behind, and Rose turned, expecting to see a customer approaching the meat counter. Instead,

Jonathan neared. His eyes were narrowed, but rather than look at her, Jonathan's eyes were fixed on Curtis. Jonathan paused at Rose's side and placed a protective hand on the small of her back. She trembled at his touch. It was not the Amish way. Jonathan's movement was bold. It reminded her that he'd seen the world, and maybe he'd picked up a few of their ways.

Jonathan fixed his gaze on hers. "Are you ready?"

Heat rose to her cheeks at his nearness.

"*Ja.*" She jutted out her chin.

Jonathan didn't withdraw his touch.

She took two steps toward the door and paused next to Curtis. "Thank you again for the cola." She thought about taking it home for her younger brother and younger sisters to try, but from the tense look on Jonathan's face she guessed that wouldn't be a good idea.

He was jealous! In a strange way it made her happy to see that.

Rose felt like she walked on a puff of air the rest of the way to the buggy.

Eleven

JONATHAN WAS QUIET AS HE HELPED HER INTO THE wagon and silent as they drove a few more blocks.

He parked at Boyd and Wurthmann Restaurant and tied up the horse. It was a small, white building with a sign that read "Home-Style Cooking." She'd only ever eaten out a few times in her life and she had to wonder what other types of cooking there were. As they entered the restaurant, she noted *Englisch*men eating lunch at back tables and Amishmen lined up along the long counter on barstools. A group of young people also sat at the green counter studying the day's pies.

They sat, and when a waitress came by they both ordered the chicken special. Rose still wasn't interested in eating, but she was starting to feel lightheaded. She handed the menu to the waitress and pressed her fingertips to her temples.

"Are you feeling all right, Rose?"

"A little lightheaded, that's all."

"Are you coming down with something?"

Rose shrugged. "Just have a lot on my mind, and I haven't had much of an appetite."

"It's my fault, isn't it?" Jonathan sighed. "All this has been hard on you, harder than I thought. He came by to talk to you, didn't he?"

Rose fiddled with the edge of the paper napkin. "Who?"

"Wallace Yoder."

"The bishop? *Ja*, he talked to me. He's been to our house several times. First after he heard you joined the military. And then when he discovered you were overseas."

"But not recently?"

"No, why?"

"He came by to talk to me last week. I assumed he took the time to get around to you too. He wanted to know what I'd been doing all that time serving in the military. I told him I worked in the field hospital, and I didn't shoot one bullet the whole time I was overseas, but it wasn't a good enough answer. He said there were more hours in a day than could be filled with tending to people. He wanted to know whom I spent time with. What I had done. He waited for me to list my sins, and he was disappointed that I wouldn't."

"He's jest considering your soul, Jonathan. He wanted to ensure you'll stay on the right path. He's our bishop—our spiritual leader."

"It's more than that, Rose, and you know it."

"I don't understand."

Jonathan lowered his head. "He believes me to be a bad influence in the community. I've experienced the world. He'd be perfectly happy if I left. We can't have anything tainting his perfect community, can we?"

"He'll change his mind about you, Jonathan. Jest give him time yet."

"I'd just assumed he'd talked to you too—recently. Why else would you think about leaving? I thought maybe he'd be an influence to keep you away from me, just like before." Jonathan reached forward, taking her hand in his. "I know what the bishop thought I should do, even before I left, but I couldn't do it. How could I sit in prison and know that men are dying when I could be helping?"

Rose leaned closer in, determined not to say anything that would hinder his outpouring.

"When the war first started, my brothers helped on the farm, and I took produce to town. I remember the day when one of the grocers refused to buy from me. *'Do you think it's fair you bring me potatoes, and I lost two boys . . . two of my boys?'* he said. I used to play with his sons when I went to the market with Dat. And I thought, how could I go to jail if I could be used to help someone else's son?" His chin quivered, bringing tears to her eyes.

"I'm sorry that I focused on the rejection I received for your choice. I should have just ignored their comments. I should have heeded no mind to their words. But I'm proud of you, Jonathan. I was here. I heard how people talked, and even then I was proud."

"You never told me that."

"I'm telling you now."

Jonathan stroked the top of her hand with his fingertips. His face glowed with those words as if she'd just given him a special gift.

"I'm glad you told me that, Rose. I've been wondering how you felt about me. You see, in my mind, in my heart, nothing has changed between us, even though you tried to push me away. If anything, my feelings for you are stronger than ever."

His eyes studied hers, and he waited for a response. Heat rose to her cheeks and she wondered if she dared confess her feelings—to spill her heart—when there were so many obstacles that would make their being together impossible.

"Are you going to answer me, Rose?"

She swallowed down her emotion. "Well . . ." She thought of the tears in Mem's eyes as she spilled the truth and wondered if Jonathan would feel the same shock.

"Do you care at all?" he asked. "Do you see any hope for our future? Can you at least answer that?"

She nodded once. "*Ja*, I wouldn't be sitting here if I didn't. I wouldn't have invited you to stay for yesterday's meal. You ought to know that."

Jonathan blew out a slow breath. He wanted her to confirm that she hadn't closed the door to thoughts of them getting married, but the more they sat, the more Rose knew she needed to tell Jonathan the whole truth. And she guessed when she did his smile would disappear.

"You'll get their favor back, you'll see," she continued. "Everyone will see your dedication. It's not like you left the Amish, left who you were born to be." The last phrase rung in her ears.

"You don't understand. Other young men from our community went to prison instead. Wallace believes that by caring for the injured soldiers I was supporting the war."

"That's foolish."

"He thinks I'm going to taint the Amish—"

"Then we don't have to worry." Rose's voice trembled.

"What do you mean?"

"Maybe this isn't the community you need to be in. Maybe there is no right community for either of us now."

"Either of us? Rose, you have done nothing to cause anyone concern. You're the most dedicated woman I know. With you—"

The waitress approached, interrupting his words. They both waited for her to put down two steaming cups of coffee before they resumed their conversation. Jonathan took a sip of his, but Rose's stomach turned just thinking of putting something to her lips. *He's going to see me differently when he knows.*

The words stuck to the roof of her mouth like Mem's peanut butter. She patted her *kapp*. "It seems the bishop doesn't want to accept you. And once they discover the truth, well, about me . . . I'm sure they will turn their back on me too."

Jonathan's jaw dropped. He roughly placed his mug down on the table and a small amount of liquid sloshed over the side.

"You aren't secretly seeing an *Englisch*man, are you?" He ran his fingers through his hair. "How could I be so stupid? The way that cashier was looking at you—"

"No!" The word shot from her lips. "I can't believe you would think that, say that. That's the first time I've seen that man. Well, at least I think it is. I would never do such a thing." Rose straightened her spine.

"Then what is it, Rose? I can see something—pain, shame—all over your face."

Fear gripped Rose's heart, but she couldn't keep it in any longer. He might reject her, but at least she wouldn't have to carry this burden alone.

"Vell, Jonathan, if you think the bishop has a problem with you . . . you just wait and see what he does with me. When he . . . when he discovers I'm not Amish."

It was hard saying the words, but with them came a relief she hadn't expected. Holding the truth in had taken more from her than she'd thought.

Jonathan's brow furrowed. "I don't understand. I know you. I've known your family for as long as I could remember. Of course you are Amish."

"It's my adopted family." Her words were no more than a whisper.

He gazed at her a moment, then chuckled and shook his head. "You're joking." When she didn't respond, he studied her face, his expression slowly dimming. "You're . . . you're not joking?"

Rose shook her head. "I—I jest found out." She expected to cry, but her soul was as frozen as the world outside. Maybe it was her way of protecting her heart. To feel numb was easier than to feel the pain of his rejection.

"Rose . . . Rose . . ." The words were like a gentle caress to her ear. "I don't know what to say. Do you trust me . . . to tell me the whole story?"

Rose placed her hand over her stomach. "*Ja*, but I'm pretty sure I won't be able to eat."

Jonathan reached forward and took her hand, squeezing it with concern. "You have to try to eat, Rose. You're looking pale . . . and thin. Even my sister mentioned how thin you've become."

When their plates of food were brought to them, Rose did her best to take a few bites, but she mostly just pushed everything around on her plate. Even Jonathan wasn't too successful at eating much of his lunch.

When Rose mustered up enough courage, she began. "I've had nightmares as long as I could remember." It was the only way she knew to start. She told him about the dreams. She told him about how Mem would come to her and would pray with her. She told Jonathan about the uneasiness she felt every winter—how she felt like she needed to do something, needed to find something. And then she told him the true story of her family.

"Mem would have most likely kept the secret forever if it hadn't been for the nightmares. And then there were good dreams too. Happy dreams that I'm starting to realize are memories."

"I never would have thought such a thing. You seem to fit in so well. They are your family. You are a part of them."

"That's the way I've always felt, but it makes me wonder . . . What would it be like if I found my real parents, my real siblings? Would I discover a part of myself that I didn't realize?"

Jonathan placed his fork on his plate and wiped the corners of his lips with a napkin. "So, are you going to find them?"

"What do you mean?"

"Your family. Are you going to find them, Rose?"

Her brows furrowed. "Why . . . that's impossible."

"Nothing's impossible. We can ask around. I'm sure there are people in Charm who remember your parents, your siblings. Maybe they know something about yer mem and dat's whereabouts."

"But what if no one knows anything? It seems like a lot of work just to be disappointed."

"Maybe you can pray—"

"Just so I can be disappointed with God too? Just to get my hopes up only to have them dashed to the ground?" She pressed her lips together and lowered her voice. "They left me, Jonathan. If they wanted me, they could have figured out a way. It's not as if Mem and Dat have gone very far. It's not as if I was the one who moved to California." The bitterness bubbling up from inside gave Rose a bad taste in her mouth. She pushed her plate away as she realized she hadn't allowed herself to feel anger toward her parents for their decision. She'd held those feelings back, but now—seeing the confusion and compassion in Jonathan's gaze—they refused to be dammed up any longer.

"But you have to find them, Rose."

"I don't have to do anything."

"*Ja*, you do. Don't you understand? You're never going to find peace or allow yerself to be part of a family . . ." Jonathan's voice trailed off. "It jest seems like a good idea to come to peace with your past before you plan your future, does it not?"

An unexpected tear moved from the corner of her eye and slid alongside her nose. "I knew you were going to say that."

"Say what?"

"Find an excuse. Say something that would push a wedge between us. Yer too good of a man to say hurtful words that would break my heart, but if you really do want to stay in this community—to regain your approval—the only way you'll be able to do that is without me. After all, you already have one strike against you, Jonathan. You don't need to add another."

"If you think being adopted by the Yoders makes you any less Amish, why that's foolish, and anyone who knows you would say the same. I wasn't telling you to make peace with your past just so I can walk away. Just the opposite. You're making too much of what I said. I can help—"

Rose lifted her hand, palm out, blocking his words.

"Don't. Please don't. Can we just finish eating and pretend I didn't tell you the truth? Can we talk about the weather and the price of pot roast?" The pain in her chest grew. "And then can you take me home?"

"If that's how it's going to be." His tone was one of sadness, tinged with anger.

"*Ja*." Rose nodded her head. "I need to think things through, Jonathan. Really think things through, and I don't need you around pulling at my heart and complicating things."

His eyes grew sad at her words, but even though she wished she could take them back, she didn't. Her life was hard enough without wondering about his place in it. And as much as she'd been excited to see him yesterday, and as much as she'd longed to have someone to talk to, releasing the truth hadn't provided what she'd hoped. No one could understand, not really.

They ate what they could of their lunch and then took a mostly silent ride home. Was the reality of who she was—what she was—finally sinking in? She'd never heard of anyone not born Amish staying and being baptized Amish. That one woman had tried and proved this to be true. The Amish heritage was one you were born into. That was that.

"I'd like you to pray about finding your family," he said as they passed the Ault place.

"I might pray . . ." She knew she would. Not that she ever would try to find them, but maybe she could come to a place of acceptance. "But even if I find them, what will that do? It won't change anything."

"You're right, Rose. Seems to me that even if you find them, you'll never really find yourself. They are only a small part of who you are. The Yoders are a part, too, but not completely. But maybe if you look to God, seek Him, then you'll find what your heart wants most of all. And maybe, when you understand His heart, you'll understand yourself a bit better too."

"Are you trying to convince me?"

"I'm trying my best."

Jonathan parked the buggy in front of her house. They sat there for a moment. Neither moved. It was as if they both wondered what to say, what to do.

The way he looked at her. Well, it was the same look he'd given her before he accepted a ride to the train station. A look that said he wasn't going to see her for a while and he wanted to remember her face.

Panic overwhelmed her. "You know, Jonathan, I just assumed we'd join the church so we could get married. I couldn't imagine ever living my life without my family and community. But now I wonder. I don't have to stay in Berlin. I wasn't born Amish. If I choose not to wear Amish dress . . . or if I buy my own vehicle, can they shun me? And you . . ." She turned and grasped the thick fabric of his jacket. "You've seen so much. You've lived out in the world. Do you really think you could be happy going back to the way things were? Do you really want to live the life of a farmer or delivery man? You could be a doctor."

"I don't want to be a doctor." Jonathan's voice was sharp. "Just because I have knowledge of the world doesn't mean I want to live there. Just because I know about medicine doesn't mean I want to practice it."

Jonathan climbed down from the wagon and offered her a hand. Instead of studying her, now he barely glanced at her. His mind was on another place—not here. Far from here. He offered her a forced smile, and she thanked him for lunch, and then without looking back she hurried down the path to the front door.

"Rose!" he called to her.

Rose paused and turned. "*Ja?*"

"Can I come back tomorrow? Can we talk again?"

She studied him for a moment, considering what tomorrow would bring. He'd talk of their future, yet also urge her to make peace with her past. He'd urge her to find her family. He'd offer to help. Though Jonathan meant well, he'd try to convince her that his way was the right one. And he'd be stuck in their Amish community. Then she'd never really know if he was staying because he believed this was the right lifestyle, or staying because he didn't want to let her go.

"No, Jonathan. I'd rather you not." Without waiting for his response, she hurried up the porch steps.

Before she'd closed the front door behind her, he was already gone. And the worst part was that Jonathan wasn't going because the world was calling him. He was going because she was pushing him away.

Twelve

THAT NIGHT ROSE PLAYED CHECKERS WITH MARTHA and then listened as Dat read the Bible in German to the family, yet her mind wasn't on the game or the words. Instead she slowly came to the realization that forcing Jonathan away hadn't started today. It had begun with the first letter she'd written to him. The one where she first declared her anger for what he had done.

Dat glanced at her when he finished reading. He paused, as if he was going to ask a question, but before he could Rose stood and moved to the kitchen to grab a candle. "I'm going to bed. I've had a headache most of the day. In fact . . . I'm not sure if I'll make it to church in the morning."

Her siblings didn't seem startled by her words, but the color washed from Mem's face.

Mem stood, knotting her hands in a ball in front of her. "Do you need me to come with you, Rose? Do you need to talk?"

Rose turned away. "*Ne*. I don't want you to catch what I have. I'd rather jest be alone." She moved down the hall to her room, not wanting to know Mem's response. Not wanting to feel the waves of pain that surely radiated from her parents. It wasn't like it was their fault. They'd done everything for her. But Rose knew that sometimes those who hurt the most were also the most innocent.

And those who were accused—like Jonathan—were also often noble . . . despite what anyone thought.

Rose placed the candle on her side table and nearly held her breath as she moved to the trunk. Jonathan's third letter was one she'd read only once, because once had been enough.

> Dear Rose,
>
> The Germans decided they weren't ready to give up. Red blood on white snow tells me that man is willing to fight for his convictions, but he's willing to fight even harder not to be shamed.
>
> One of my jobs is to clean wounds and wrap bandages. The medical reason is to stop infections, but bandages also hide the wounds that no one wants to see.
>
> It's hard work, but to get me through I think of you. I think of returning to you. I think of your smile. I know I should pray yet, but prayer reminds me of the problems. Instead, thoughts of you make me think past the problems to the future.

Jonathan had stopped there. He must have come back and finished the letter at a different time. The ink looked different. The script looked different. And the words—well, she had no doubt what had happened. In between the first and second part of his letter, her own had arrived. The one where she'd poured out her pain and anger. She'd wondered how he could have done this to her. He had escaped, but she was the one living in the community. The one who heard the disapproval of the bishop. Who lived with the stares of church members.

She had been ashamed. It had been winter and the darkness had descended on her soul. Along with that, feelings of emptiness and of missing Jonathan. Rose couldn't remember everything she'd written, but it was clear that her fears had shouted louder than hope's whispers.

She'd been selfish, she realized now. She'd shown Jonathan her wounds, but had given him no way to bandage them up. She could see now that his words meant to do that, but they fell short.

> I received your letter, Rose. I won't lie and tell you that even though you feel as you do I'm confident we'll make it through this. I'm not. Men die that should be able to pull through, and those who I'm certain have no fighting chance keep on fighting. When I weighed joining and leaving and coming home, I thought we would pull through. But now I'm not so sure.
>
> You tell me you love me, and I believe that. If it wasn't for love, then your emotions wouldn't be so strong. Those strong emotions are the only thing that give me hope. A wound hurts more from a friend than an enemy. My leaving hurts more because your heart

has already attached itself to mine. And because of that I'll keep writing you. And because of that you'll keep reading the letters I send. And maybe when I'm set to return and I write to tell you that I do want to marry you, the strong pain will remind you of my strong love and we'll be able to move past this and struggle to fit into the community we both love, despite what you see as my great betrayal.

Jonathan

Rose folded the letter and set it on the side table. He'd returned but nothing had gotten better. Maybe if they'd only had to deal with his status in their community they could have overcome this together. Now? It seemed impossible.

Lord, is there any glimmer of hope I can cling to? Any at all?

THE MEMORIES SCROLLED THROUGH JONATHAN'S MIND, as they did every night. They never played out in order—flashes of images, of emotions, of fears. Tall trees with heavy limbs covered in snow in the woods near Bastogne. The bombed-out German villages with frightened faces peering out the windows. The white crosses near the shores of Normandy. The camps in Austria. It was hard tending injured soldiers. Harder still was tending sores on thin bodies draped in black-and-white-striped uniforms and questioning if it was any good. Many concentration camp victims had been so thin he could lift grown men like children. Yet the former prisoners had at least died seeing faces of compassion gazing upon them. That had eased his own pain from not being able to do enough. Never enough.

Jonathan turned to his side on his feather bed and pulled his mem's thick quilt over his shoulders. He hadn't shared much of what he'd seen and experienced. He'd told his dat a few things, but noting how uncomfortable it made his father, he'd stopped. Why would people want to hear stories like that? Wasn't it enough that he'd come back? Wasn't it enough that they'd won the war?

His stomach ached, but he wasn't coming down with something. The pain came from Rose's news. His heart ached for her truth. His stomach ached, knowing what he'd have to do to help her face it.

He couldn't care less that she wasn't born Amish. Rose was as *gut* an Amish woman as any he'd met. He had no doubt that they would get married and follow the way of their ancestors—if not in this community then another. What bothered him were the questions that filled her eyes. They were the same questions he'd seen in the internment camps.

Where are they?

What happened?

Do they still think of me?

Am I not forgotten?

More than food, the prisoners had wanted answers. What had happened on the outside? Did anyone know the whereabouts of their family? When could they leave and try to find their loved ones? Lack of food shriveled up a body, but lack of answers, of truth, ate at one's mind. There were men who every day spoke of finding a wife or child. Jonathan only hoped they had.

If he was ever going to be able to ask for Rose's hand in marriage—her whole heart—he'd have to find answers for her first. Even sad news was better than not knowing.

The only way to gain Rose in the end was to walk away from her now . . . and seek the answers she was too afraid to search for.

Lord, give me strength.

Thirteen

ROSE FELT STRANGE WEARING HER EVERYDAY CLOTHES while everyone else donned their Sunday best. She had only missed church service a few times that she could remember—once when she was ill and two other times when she stayed home to be with Mem after the birth of a sibling.

Little Martha's shoulders drooped as she approached. "Are you sure you don't want to come, Rose?"

"I'm sure I'll be feeling better next time around." Rose offered what she hoped was an eager smile. "I do hate to miss it."

Dat walked past her and offered a sideways glance as he slid on his coat. He moved toward the door and then paused, approaching Rose. He placed a hand on her shoulder and a thin layer of tears filled his eyes.

"If you need to talk, I'm here, *ja?*"

She nodded and placed her hand over his. "*Danki*. Thank you, Dat. Thank you for everything."

He stepped away, removed his hat from the peg on the wall, and set it firmly on his head, then walked with quickened steps out to the barn to finish hitching up the buggy.

He was obviously concerned, but she could tell he didn't think any less of her than he had days ago. He didn't seem too bothered that she'd chosen to stay home. Mem said Dat's mind was always at work. Even when his body sat, his mind was never still. Maybe he—more than anyone—understood that she needed time to think before facing their community.

Mem approached next and placed a soft hand on Rose's cheek. "We'll be back before long, *ja*? We'll see you then. I do hope you start feeling better soon."

Louisa wrapped her arms around Rose's legs and clung tight. Rose gently patted her sister's *kapp*. "I'll be here when you return. I'm not going anywhere."

Louisa lifted her chin and rested it on Rose's stomach. Her youngest sisters's lip puckered and her wide-eyed gaze didn't look convinced. Louisa was a sensitive one. She no doubt realized from Dat's and Mem's actions that more was going on than just Rose not feeling well.

"Then tonight I'll read you another chapter of *Heidi*, *ja*?" Rose offered. "Maybe we'll read the chapter of Heidi and Grandmother again . . . but I'll save the new chapter for everyone at school."

A few minutes later, her family piled into the buggy, placing blankets around each other. She imagined their bodies pressed together and how the heated stones Mem had tucked into coat pockets would warm them up by the time they got to the end of the lane.

Five minutes later the buggy's wheels creaked over the gravel and her siblings' voices bounced across the frozen ground. And then another minute after that, the world seemed void of all sound. Only the crackling of the fire told her that she hadn't slipped into nothingness.

The silence of the house penetrated her heart. Rose blinked hard, trying to clear her vision, but the image of the buggy blurred as it crested the hill and disappeared.

She turned away from the window and wiped her eyes with her palms, running her hands down her face as she sat. She allowed tears to wash her cheeks. It was hard staying home, but she couldn't imagine walking into the church service, looking around and questioning who knew. Surely those who'd lived in Berlin most of their lives knew the truth. Those who'd been Mem and Dat's friends . . . and who'd possibly known her *Englisch* parents. Had members of her own community spoken about her in hushed tones whenever she wasn't in earshot? Had they shared the story with their children? Had everyone in the community known but her?

A trembling hand covered her stomach, and her breakfast felt like a lump. Had she been a laughingstock among them? "*Look at Rose, trying to be the perfect Amish woman. If she only knew the truth . . .* "

Truth.

What was the truth? That her birth parents had abandoned her? Not her other siblings, but *her*. What had she done so wrong to not be worthy of their love?

I love you . . . The voice floated through her mind, as soft as a butterfly landing on her fingertip. In the past she'd trusted it was God's voice, but what did she know?

Then again, what did she have without Him? Where could she turn except to God? She needed Him, more now than ever.

She sat in Mem's rocker and attempted to work on her tatting, but her mind couldn't concentrate enough to count the stitches. Instead she rose and set the table for supper. Tin cups, chipped ceramic plates. For as long as she could remember their family had never had new things. Their clothes and shoes came from cousins. There was always just enough to eat . . . and the jars of canned food sometimes ran out before winter did. Yet Mem and Dat always had enough to go around. It made her sad to consider how poor her birth family had been then, to not even have what she'd grown up with here. What if they were still in need now? Tears filled her eyes and she blinked them away. How could she ever enjoy life without knowing if they still went to bed hungry at night?

The hours passed slowly, and Rose watched out the window for her family to return. Finally their buggy crested the hill. An even greater joy—her brother-in-law and sister's buggy followed.

Excited voices entered the house, and little Louisa seemed especially excited to see Rose, but it was Vera's pinched face that drew Rose's attention. And when Vera took the cradle to Rose's room to lay baby Ira down for a nap, Rose followed.

Vera spoke about the church service and the low attendance because of the weather. She shared news of new couples dating, but Rose could tell that's not what she really wanted to talk about. Rose waited as Vera changed the baby's diaper, swaddled him, and then placed him in the crib. Then, with her lower lip turned down, and large mournful eyes, Vera turned to Rose.

"I think Jonathan might be considering leaving . . ." Vera fiddled with the strings of her *kapp*.

"Leaving?" Even though Rose thought it could happen—that Jonathan would go elsewhere—she was surprised. "Where is he going?"

"You don't understand. Leaving the Amish."

The air punched out of Rose as if a bridle tightened around her lungs. She sat. "Why would you think that?"

Vera lowered her head. Red burned her sister's cheeks.

"Did he tell you something?"

"*Ne*, I saw something. He was in a vehicle, in town. With a woman."

A trembling hand touched Rose's lips. She had done this. She'd given Jonathan enough reason to walk away. When he'd asked to come back and talk to her, she'd told him not to. Even though she'd done this to herself, pain ripped at her heart.

"Who was she? Was it someone from Berlin?"

"I don't know. I'm not sure. I do not think I recognized her. We'd gone to church at the Bontragers' house and we were driving back through town. I tried to get a good look while we passed, but the woman's face was turned away from the buggy. She was focused on Jonathan."

"Did they look . . . close?"

It wasn't until Vera answered that Rose realized she'd asked the question out loud.

"I'm not sure . . . They were focused on each other, as if they were deep in conversation. I'm sorry, Rose. I know you have so many questions. There has been so much on your mind lately. I'm sorry to add another question. I just thought you would want to know."

"Did I?" Rose turned away. She crossed her arms over her chest. She'd been so sad about it all. She'd been overwhelmed with questions about the past. About the future. But now an unwelcome emotion returned: anger.

Rose stood, shaking. "Did I want to know that? No. Did I want to know that I was abandoned by my real parents? No. This is not how my life was supposed to be. Why couldn't have things been as I'd always thought? I never wanted anything different than what I already had." Her voice lowered. "I had everything . . . or so I thought."

"Did you, Rose? Was life perfect? Do you really think so?"

"*Ja*. Did you think it wasn't?"

"I am your sister. I saw the fear in your eyes. I saw the questions. You say you didn't know . . . but deep down, somewhere, you wondered about your life. It was as if you walked through each day in your normal routine, but you were trying to figure it out."

"Figure out what?"

"You tell me that."

Rose held her elbows tight at her sides. She had no control of anything anymore, especially now with the pounding of her heart and the tightness of her lungs. During the war everything had been uncertain. Every day they'd waited for the news. Is that what had brought the uncertainty? Had she been used to waiting for bad news—looking for trouble? Is that what had caused the tension deep inside? Or was it something more?

Oh, Lord, I don't know what to think anymore. My life feels as if I'm on a runaway stallion, and I don't know how to make it stop . . . how to just make everything stop.

Fourteen

ROSE FOUND HERSELF HEADING TO TOWN THE NEXT Friday after reading another chapter of *Heidi* to the children at school. Chapter twelve had always been one of her favorites. Even the children who knew the story—who had heard it last year—had grown tense and still as Rose read about the ghost in Clara's house. They sat at the edges of their seats as if they were waiting to discover there was no ghost at all, but rather Heidi sleepwalking. The words Rose had read were still on her mind as she entered Hummel's Grocery after catching a ride to town with Dat.

"*Yes, I dream every night, and always about the same things,*" Heidi had told the doctor who'd come to see her. "*I think I am back with Grandfather and I hear the sound in the fir trees outside, and I see the stars shining so brightly, and then I open the door quickly and run out, and it is all so beautiful! But when I wake I am still in Frankfurt.*"

"*And have you no pain anywhere? No pain in your head or back?*" the doctor had asked Heidi.

Her answer was one Rose understood. "*No, only a feeling as if there were a great stone weighing on me here.*"

"As if you had eaten something that would not go down."

"No, not like that; something heavy as if I wanted to cry very much."

Rose wiped away a tear, entered the grocery store, and noticed Curtis at the front register. He was just finishing up with a customer. Curtis bagged up the last of the woman's items and wished her well. As the woman moved toward the door, Rose approached the cashier.

He lifted an eyebrow, and concern filled his face. "Can I help you with something? You don't look too well, Rose."

"I was just looking for Jonathan. I haven't heard from him in a few days. Is he still working in the back storeroom, building those shelves?"

"Your Jonathan?" The man waved a hand. "Nah. I thought you of all people knew he'd left town. Said he had very important business, although he didn't tell me what." He scratched his head. "It didn't have something to do with you, miss, did it? I should have asked. I should have told Jonathan that I'd be willing to help you both. That Curtis Williams is always willing to help a friend."

"That's kind of you." She forced a smile. "I'm afraid he didn't talk to me about it." She turned her back to Curtis and stared out the window as if somehow by chance she'd see Jonathan walking down the street. "It seems he has a habit of that—of leaving first and telling me what's really going on later."

Rose felt a hand on her arm and jumped. How inappropriate! She pulled away from Curtis's touch and was about to give the man a piece of her mind when she noticed the compassion on his face. Just seeing it made her realize he simply wanted to be a friend—to be there for her.

"I'm sorry. Didn't mean to scare you none. I know since I'm new around here, folks don't know what to think of me, but I'd like to be known around here as a trustworthy fellow. If there is ever anything I could do to help—"

"There is." The words slipped out before she could stop them. "I have a friend—a neighbor. He's also a returning soldier." She glanced down at Curtis's cane. "Harold was injured, but in other ways. He's not handling everything so well. It's his mind that plays tricks on him. It seems that there are days he feels he's more *there* than here."

Curtis nodded, seeming to understand.

"If you could . . ."

"You'd like me to go visit him?"

"*Ja*, if it wouldn't be too much."

Curtis ran a hand down his cheek. "I've talked to a few other soldiers around here, but none of them want to talk much. I don't know—"

"Harold might not want to talk, but I'm sure he'd appreciate the visit. Even more, I think his parents would. Jonathan stopped by once and it helped a lot."

Curtis nodded. "If you don't think they'll mind."

"Not at all."

"Then I can do it tomorrow."

She glanced on the counter for a piece of paper. "*Danki*. I can write down the address."

"No need. I know the Ault place." He noted her surprise. "It's a small community."

"*Ja*, I suppose, although I'm not sure I've even been down every road."

Curtis chuckled. "I have, uh, a car . . . my first. I enjoy driving the roads. I know where many folks live. I guess you can just say I'm trying to get to know my community better."

"I understand." Still, Rose couldn't help but feel this man was acting very kindly toward her, a mere stranger. Something wasn't right about Curtis Williams. He didn't quite seem to fit into this town—and yet he was working hard to *make* himself fit . . .

The hair on the back of her neck pricked as Rose offered another thank-you and turned to find a shopping basket. She hoped Dat wouldn't take too long with his errands.

Beginning to fill her basket, Rose turned to something that worried her more—the information Curtis had given her. Jonathan was gone. Was he gone for good? Surely his parents would hear from him. Maybe she should try to contact him through them.

Rose decided when she got home she'd write a letter and take it by his parents' house. He couldn't leave them all . . . not for good. And when Jonathan returned she wanted him to know her heart: if she had any chance of a relationship with Jonathan, it was time to let the future matter more than the past. She just hoped that God would help make that so.

Dear Jonathan,

You left. You really left. Not that I blame you. I understand why you did, because ever since I saw your letter with the postmark from France, I feared my love wouldn't be enough to hold you to Berlin, hold you to being Amish. How could one see the world, see all the possibilities, and then return and live life within two square miles?

And yet the thing about fear is that in the back of your mind you're trying to convince yourself it's not really there. Like when I'd wake up from my dreams—my nightmares—as a child. With my heart pounding in the dark, my safe bedroom no longer felt safe. Even with Vera sleeping beside me with a warm body and soft breaths, the room itself turned against me. The shadow in the corner was a stray dog, waiting to pounce. The rattle of my window a thief ready to break in. But I'd tell myself that it was just a shadow, just the wind, until I could relax enough to fall asleep.

I was so certain you'd leave, and then I dared to have hope. On Thanksgiving Day—and the few days that followed—I tried to tell myself maybe you would stay.

Yet the shadow in the corner was a thief this time, and you are gone. Did I open the door and let him in with my fears? Or did discovering the truth of my life make you realize there really isn't anything worth staying around Berlin for? One person's scandal is enough to set us at the edge of the community, but I know—and you know—that both of our stories match us for each other, but set us apart from the simple people around us who don't realize that perhaps their greatest gift is belonging.

Mem's words—the truth—were a surprise, but also a confirmation. I've always felt different, even when I thought I belonged. I knew there was a reason Marcus treated me as someone special. It was like the time we took Elizabeth to the hospital when she was seven with a big gash in her leg. The nurse doted on her and gave her candy as they waited for the doctor, and even while Elizabeth accepted it and smiled, her eyes held fear because she knew their niceness was for a reason. The stitches were the reason.

Why am I writing all this? Why now? Because just as I always carry around a little bit of fear, I also carry around a little bit of hope. When you returned—and I spoke harsh words to you—the hope was that you'd come to me, find me, and tell me that you would stay, that I was worth staying for. And you did come. On Thanksgiving Day—the morning after I'd heard the hard news—your arrival meant that you were going to fight for the feelings that I also felt. And writing this letter, and leaving it on your pillow, means that hope is there that you will return.

Differences set you apart, but difference also makes you special, like Marcus continues to show me. My story is different than everyone else's in Berlin. Your story is different. But if love can find a way through this, and if truth can pull together instead of push apart, and if we can get to a place where our prayers tell God that we are thankful He didn't answer our petitions like we thought we wanted, then I think we'll have something special that most couples won't have. We'll have fought and won, where they've just accepted and melded.

Love, Rose

Fifteen

THE NEXT TIME MARCUS AND KATIE CAME OVER, Marcus's beard had come in fully, and from the glow on Katie's face Rose expected that in a few months the couple would make it known a new member was joining their family.

Elizabeth had brought out her colored pencils and paper, and they sat around the kitchen table, making Christmas cards to mail to friends who lived out of town.

Sitting next to Katie, Rose couldn't help but consider her own mother. Had she and her father been excited to know they were expecting her? Were they pleased it was a girl? She pretended they did. She imagined her mother snuggling her close after her birth, breathing in her scent, and forgetting the family's lack of means.

On the paper before her, she drew a candle and a bunch of holly, wondering what her other parents and siblings were doing. She circled a freshly sharpened red pencil on the page, making berries on the holly, wishing she had a way to send them a card. But who could even begin to guess where they'd ended up.

"I'm going to town in the morning if anyone would like to go," Marcus interrupted her thoughts.

"I would," Rose spoke up. She looked at her brother, studying his face, hoping he'd go along with her plan.

It had been weeks since she'd been to town, weeks since Jonathan had left, and weeks since she'd seen the cashier Curtis—although Mrs. Ault had stopped over twice, telling them what a good friend "that Williams boy" had become. It helped to have someone who understood the war in the South Pacific—someone Harold could talk to who wasn't rattled by his injured mind.

It had also been weeks since she'd written her letter to Jonathan, although it still sat on top of her linens.

"That was a quick answer, Rose." Mem looked up at her from her quilting, surprised. "Do you have shopping to do?"

"You can say that." Her mind scurried for a reason, but she could come up with none. Her eyes met with Marcus's. Night after night she'd lain in bed and heard Jonathan's words: "*You need to find peace with your past, Rose.*" Out of everyone, she knew that Marcus would help make that possible. Her older brother had always been there for her, and she knew he'd be there again when she asked him to take her to Charm.

"Rose, do you have Nancy Shank's new address? Last I heard, they'd moved to Somerset County," Elizabeth asked.

Rose set down the colored pencil. "*Ja.*"

"Stay where you are. I can get it." Elizabeth jumped to her feet. "Is it in your trunk?"

"Yes. It should be right on top."

Without a moment's hesitation Elizabeth darted off.

Rose finished her card and wrote a short note to her pen pal, also named Rose, who lived in the next community over. *Dear Rose, I do think of you. I miss your smile. I can't wait to see you again, and if I don't talk to you, have a good new year too. I know God has good plans for you in the coming months.*

And for a moment, as Rose looked over her handiwork, she pretended that note had been for her. That someone special had left it. That someone couldn't get her off his mind.

THE NEXT MORNING MARCUS WAS DRESSED AND SIPPING a cup of coffee by the time Rose entered the living room. Dat was in the barn choring, the kids were readying for school, and Mem and Katie had plans to piece together a new quilt.

Rose grabbed a plate and a fresh biscuit. She didn't bother with putting on jam or butter. Instead she took a big bite, eager to get the day started. "I do have to do some Christmas shopping too."

"Too?" He lowered his chin and looked down at her, peering into her eyes. "Do you mean on our way back from Charm?"

Rose put down her biscuit. She crossed her arms over her chest again, feeling as if everyone knew the truth—saw the truth—better than her. Pushing back from the table, she moved to the kitchen window, looking out at the frozen earth. In the distance she saw a car driving slowly—too slowly—past their house. She sucked in a breath as she realized who it was. *Curtis*. Again an uneasy feeling swept over her. Her heartbeat quickened and worries filled her mind. What did they know about this man? Why had he taken such an interest in their community? Her heartbeat stilled only as she watched his car pull into the Ault place and park.

You have too active an imagination, she told herself. *He's just trying to find friends in this new place. That's all.*

"That is where you wanted to go, Rose, isn't it? To Charm?"

Rose turned back to Marcus and noted compassion on her brother's face. "How did you know what I was going to ask?"

"You've been here, but you haven't been present. I've been wondering when you'd ask someone to drive you by the old place. And since Jonathan left town, I've been expecting that you'd ask me. Everyone has been wondering what's wrong. Dat and Mem can't get up the nerve to tell the younger kids. Still, they are worried. We all love you, Rose. I wish we could help you somehow—give you the answer you are waiting for. But like Katie said, it's a journey that you'll have to take on your own."

Rose's fists clenched as she thought of Jonathan. Marcus was right. If Jonathan had stayed, she would have asked him. But Rose didn't want to consider that, think about that. She pushed out her bottom lip.

"Katie knows?"

"She was worried about you. She kept telling me that something was wrong. She insisted you needed to get into the doctor, that you had a disease."

"Being *Englisch* isn't contagious."

"You're not *Englisch*, Rose. At least not anymore. And besides, I think you could say that anything you allow to eat you away inside can be considered a disease."

ROSE AND MARCUS CHATTED ABOUT EVERYDAY THINGS as Marcus drove the buggy the six miles to Charm. The horse's breath blew out in a gentle rhythm. While her childhood memories were piecemeal, Marcus was older. He remembered more, no doubt. She wanted to ask about her family but was afraid maybe her longing would grow.

He turned down a side road and they passed two farms. Around a corner another farm stood. A buggy was parked out front. The barn door was open and white curtains hung in the windows of the house. The place looked warm and inviting. Rose cocked her head. It also looked familiar. As they neared the house both of them fell silent.

Finally the words bunched in her throat, but she pushed them out. "Mem and Dat's place?"

"*Ja*." It was a simple response. Then his gaze moved past the Amish farm to the next piece of property. She followed it. There was the orchard that she remembered in foggiest detail. And beyond it a smaller house that had seen better years. It was an abandoned, ramshackle place. Rose wondered who owned the land now. There were many such places around their community. During the Depression, when families could no longer pay for their property, they'd often just walked away.

She held her breath as the buggy neared and leaned forward to get a better view. She waited for the moment that something would click, the moment the memories would flood back. But even as the buggy approached and parked on the small turnout, nothing came.

Rose looked at the faded gray structure, sure it would blow down with every gust of wind. Still it stood, despite its state of disrepair. A small porch shielded the front door set off by two windows.

Above the porch roof sat two more windows—maybe from some type of loft. At least a quarter of the shingles were missing, the dark spots reminding her of Louisa's smile with her missing teeth. A wooden fence with chicken-wire protected the property—or, rather, became a gathering point for musty, decaying leaves. A tree, thin and scraggly, stretched gray limbs into the sky.

Does it bloom in spring? If so, it had to be the only form of life around this place.

Even the ground in the fields beyond the house looked scraped away, as if the wind had stripped it of all topsoil. Rose cautiously stepped toward the house over a thin layer of snow and ice. In her mind's eye she pictured the single gable-end chimney breathing out puffs of smoke like the dragon books Marcus used to read. She pictured the gray boards as fresh lumber. The windows gleaming and framed with curtains, and a family with smiles and hope—lots of hope—sitting inside. Now, though, it was only a broken-down shell of its former glory.

"Would you like me to come with you?" Marcus's voice called to her.

Rose glanced back, almost forgetting for a moment he was with her. "Can you give me five minutes?"

"*Ja*. Of course."

Rose walked toward the porch and paused at the steps. She gripped the banister, partly to make sure she didn't step on any of the rotten boards, and partly because she needed strength to continue on.

On the porch she attempted to peek in the window, but the glass was dingy and it was too dark to see anything much inside. She moved to the door and noticed the screen had been ripped off its hinges. Her hand moved to the knob, and she expected it to be locked. Instead the knob turned with ease and the door swung open.

"Dear Lord . . . ," she whispered, unsure of what to pray for. Tears gathered in her eyes, and she dabbed at them.

A layer of dust covered the warped floorboards and everything inside sat so still, so silent. There was a chair without a back and a small table that had seen better days.

She looked out the side window, noticing the springhouse, the barn, and the orchard stripped bare and lifeless. Her soul felt the same. To go from belonging and feeling a part of a family and a community to being an outsider rubbed her heart raw, as if someone had peeled off the top layer with a paring knife.

"Did Jonathan feel the same after how I treated him?" she whispered, her breath condensing on the dirty window glass. He'd been out of the community, not only living in a different state but on the other side of the world. And yet he came back ready to leave the past behind him. He was braver than she'd thought; he'd risked more than just his life. He'd made an effort to move beyond the past too. Why couldn't she do the same? What was holding her back? She'd faced much less than the horror of war. And he'd only done what his conscience deemed right. Yet she'd blamed him for her unhappiness—allowed the bishop and neighbors' attitudes to poison her own.

Rose felt like a fool now. What would have happened if she had encouraged him, stood up for him? What would have happened if she'd listened to him and had asked him to help her make peace with her past? Would he have stayed? She'd finally confessed her need in a letter, but what good did it do sitting in her trunk? Why did it take such a dreary day, in the midst of all she'd lost, to see so clearly?

If only he were still here, she'd tell him.

She heard the door creak open behind her and turned. Marcus entered with slow steps, and she waved him in, thankful for his presence.

"Your mem had a beautiful garden out back. Even when the dust was thick and nothing would grow, her little rose garden thrived. Mem said it grew on hope and leftover dishwater. Dat said if Betty would have been as mindful about a vegetable garden, they might not be in such a pickle. She had a collection of vases, and she'd fill them with roses . . . and wild daisies."

Rose smiled, thinking about that, but it also made her

sad to consider her mother's loss. First Daisy to death, and then Rose to . . . circumstances? Fear of the same?

"Mem used to click her tongue after a visit to your parents' house. 'Cut flowers!' she'd exclaim. 'They'd live longer if they remained in God's good earth where He planted them.' Yet I remember one week when Dat had gone to Indiana to help his cousin raise a barn and Mem gathered a bunch of wildflowers and set them in a jelly jar on the counter. *Ach*, I thought her eyes were gonna turn pink and purple and blue for the amount of staring she did on those. But they were gone by the time Dat came home, and she never allowed herself the pleasure again."

"She . . . enjoyed their beauty?"

"*Ja*."

"And I jest thought all this time that she disapproved of my decorating."

"Haven't you seen her gazing upon the greenery, the flowers, the pinecones and small plants? I bring those things for her as much as you, Rose. You've brought a *gut* beauty into our lives. A *gut* beauty." Marcus sighed audibly. "You see, Dat thought your family needed a garden for food . . . and they did. But flowers feed our soul in a different way. They remind us of a God who creates beautiful things and takes notice of the tiniest detail."

Did her mother still garden? Did she still love her roses best?

"You look like her, too, especially when you do that."

"Do what?"

"Tilt your head when you're thinking. I'd see your mem standing out by the clothesline sometimes. She wouldn't be working, but instead just enjoying the view of the orchard or fields, her head cocked and her mind in another place. *Ja*, you look like her, all right."

Rose touched her hand to her cheek. "I do?"

He nodded. "She had long, blonde hair that fell down her back. I'd watch it move when she walked because Mem's hair was never like that."

There were steps heading up to a loft and Marcus sat on them. The light from the window lit the front area, but Rose had no desire to look into the other rooms. She'd seen them enough times in her nightmares. Why would she want to peer into their murky darkness?

Marcus looked around. "Your mem used to have yellow curtains in that window and all sorts of pretty things around. I remember that because it looked so different from our place. And so many colors. A red tablecloth, a blue vase, some paintings on the wall—maybe ones she did herself. I've always thought that's where you got yer love of pretty things."

"I never knew." Rose wanted to ask more, but just that one thought was enough to carry around and turn over in her mind for a while. Instead she headed to the front door.

Marcus heaved himself off the step. They exited, and she paused on the porch. Tears filled her eyes.

"They did it to save you, Rose. They did it because of love. After Daisy died . . . well, this place was gloomy, even with all the bright colors. And when you became sick . . ."

He released a sigh. "I know they thought you were next. I know their decision meant you had a chance to live—to have a good life. I have no doubt."

She nodded and a fresh breath of warmth touched the edges of her heart.

"It's getting dark," he said. "Looks like a storm's coming in."

Rose wanted to cry at the thought of leaving, but instead an unexpected emotion came over her: thankfulness. She was thankful for the family who'd lived here. Thankful that the Yoders happened to be their neighbors. Thankful she'd survived and was standing here now.

She glanced toward the orchard again as they walked toward the buggy. Yes, the trees were stripped bare, but in four months they'd be blooming with life. All the trees needed for growth, for fruit, was tucked inside—the Creator God made sure of that. She had to believe God had good plans tucked deep inside her too.

She accepted Marcus's hand as he helped her into the buggy, and she didn't look back as they drove away. It wasn't needed. Everything she'd seen would be carried close to her heart.

Sixteen

THE STORM HAD COME IN QUICKER THAN THEY'D HOPED, slowing their progress on the six-mile trip back to Berlin, slowing their progress around town, and chilling Rose to the core. By the time she and Marcus returned from their errands and shopping, the day was gone and the others had already eaten dinner. Dat had sent the children to bed early, and Katie was ready to travel home with Marcus. Elizabeth sat at the table sketching a picture. She barely glanced up at Rose when she entered, but she had a sly look on her face. Rose guessed that she and Mem had made or wrapped Rose's Christmas present that day. Elizabeth had never been one to conceal her emotions. Once when she was little, Elizabeth had found everyone's presents and had taken them to them, laying them on their pillows a week prior to Christmas because she couldn't handle the suspense. She hadn't changed much, and Rose noticed the twinkle in Elizabeth's eye as she kissed Rose's cheek and bid her goodnight.

As soon as Marcus ate, he and Katie hurried out of the house. He still had choring to do and the minutes were ticking by. Soon only Dat and Rose sat before the fire.

"*Hungerich?*"

She was hungry, but she didn't feel like eating. It seemed too much work.

"Where's Mem?" she asked.

"Feeling under the weather."

"I'm the cause of that, aren't I?"

"She has a tender heart, Rose. She aches for you."

"I feel so bad." Rose released a breath. "It's not that I don't appreciate what you've done."

He rubbed the side of his face. "What we've done?"

"The sacrifice to take me in. To share your Amish heritage." Her stomach growled, but she ignored it. She rubbed it, willing it to calm its angry rumbles.

He pointed to the kitchen. A loaf of bread sat on the wooden countertop. "Eat something, Rose, please. I never did like seeing you hungry."

It was only after she'd cut herself a slice of bread and returned to the chair that he turned his attention to her again.

"What you think is a sacrifice I consider a gift. God's gift. Children are a gift from the Lord, and the way you came to us makes you more special." Dat stroked the long beard that fell to his second button. "I feel like Joseph at times."

"Joseph?"

"*Ja*, Jesus's father from the Bible. He was given a child to raise that wasn't his own. It's an honor. Every time that God gives us a child, it's His way of saying He trusts us—trusts us to offer love and to guide the child toward Him."

Rose hadn't heard her dat talk this way very often. Though he read from the Scriptures, he rarely talked about what was really happening deep inside his heart—most Amish men didn't. She leaned forward in her rocking chair, as if his words were a golden cord drawing her closer.

"I've wanted to tell you sooner, Rose. Maybe I should have tried. Mem didn't want to hurt you, but I believe waiting hurt you more. God chose us to raise you. I've been confident that He's always intended you to be Amish." He paused. "It was by the hand of God that your parents were our neighbors. It was by His hand that they learned to trust us."

"I'm not so sure . . . I wasn't born Amish. If God had wanted me to be part of an Amish family, wouldn't He have just had me born into an Amish home?"

"Maybe He wanted you to be a part of *two* families' hearts." Dat lowered his head and glanced at her over the rim of his reading glasses, but although she wanted to believe him—trust his words—her heart still ached.

"Do you think that you are the only one who benefited, Rose? That it was a duty or a chore to care for you, love you? You were a gift to us. My heart wrapped around you just as much as the others. Maybe more. The Bible says we are adopted as sons and daughters into God's kingdom. Having you in our family has helped me to understand more what a beautiful gift that is."

"*Ja*." Dat's words were true—she knew they were. Rose just wished her heart believed them. "But what about my future, Dat? Where do I go from here?"

"It seems to me, Rose, the kind of ancestors you have is not as important as the ones your children have." He released a heavy sigh. "God has let this day dawn, *liebling* . . . just as He gave us the day when you joined our family. We must thank Him for it, and ask Him for our purpose in it."

"I always seemed to know my purpose before: to become an Amish wife and mother. All my life I looked forward to one thing," she offered with a sigh.

"What's that?"

"My Amish wedding. Thinking about it. Planting the celery in the spring, knowing that it'll grace the tables after harvest. Seeing everyone gathered there to celebrate my joy."

"You don't think it'll happen? Jest because Jonathan left doesn't mean he's gone for good. Or maybe another young man . . ."

Rose shook her head. She couldn't think of marrying anyone else. She couldn't think of ever hoping Jonathan would come back. What was here for him?

"Even if there was someone, Dat, do you think the bishop would allow it . . . once he discovers the truth of who I am?"

Dat rocked back and forth in his chair. "The bishop knows you, Rose. Surely he'll take your heart that loves God, and your commitment to our Amish ways, into consideration."

"Maybe Jonathan made the right choice." Her words were barely a whisper. "Maybe leaving, starting over, is the one way to be welcomed into a community, accepted, once everyone knows the truth."

Rose stood and walked over to her dat. Leaning down,

she kissed his cheek before quickly hurrying away. She'd never shown Dat affection like that, but what did it matter now? Especially if she was going to leave.

In her room, Rose lit the candle on her side table, and her shoulders quivered slightly as she noticed a brown-wrapped package on the trunk. Attached to it was a note:

Dear Rose,

This is the package that your parents left to you. It tells me that they wanted you to know you'd always be a part of their family. Part of my heart doesn't want to share you—my love for you is as high as the stars. But the other part of me knows that you were on loan to us.

I trust you, Rose, to follow God wherever He leads. Know that discovering who God designed you to be won't make us love you any less. Know that you always have a home with us, as long as you choose. Know I have cherished each day as your mother. Even as I looked at you, I hurt for those who didn't get to experience raising you. I have prayed for your family, Rose. I've prayed they would always follow God and that He would heal their hearts that might be missing you.

Dear girl, please forgive me for waiting so long to give you this gift. I wanted to hold you a little longer, but now it's time to bloom, Rose, and to grace the world with the beauty and fragrance God has planned all along.

Love, Mem

With trembling hands Rose opened the package. White cloth was tucked inside. Rose opened it and unfolded it slowly, feeling the softness of the cotton flour sack.

A gasp escaped her lips. It was the apron—the one Louisa had brought into the kitchen all those weeks ago. So it wasn't a Christmas gift . . . well, at least not from Mem. She imagined her mother—her birth mother—holding this object. Goosebumps rose on her arms.

Twenty yellow roses were embroidered on the front so they made a ring along the bottom near the hem. Rose brushed her hands across them. The vibrant color had not faded. The thread was surely as bright as it had been all those years ago.

She turned it over and noticed more small stitching. She gasped, her mouth an O.

"The names of my family."

- Stan Williams—father
- Betty Williams—mother
- Timothy Williams—brother
- Curtis Williams—brother
- Rose Williams
- Daisy Williams—sister, RIP

Curtis Williams? Rose sat straighter with a start. It was the name of the grocery store clerk . . . the one she'd found so friendly. Could that be her brother?

And what if he was? Did he know? Had he come back to the area for a reason? Rose had to ask him.

But not yet.

"I can't," she whispered. Not until after Christmas, at least. She couldn't think about leaving until after then.

Rose folded up the apron and tucked it deep into her wooden chest next to Jonathan's letters.

"I just want one more Christmas to enjoy my family," she whispered. "Dear God . . . I don't know what I'm supposed to do after that, but can You make this Christmas special, memorable?"

And as Rose closed her wooden chest, an eagerness filled her. She couldn't wait until morning to talk to Mem. Her mother's love had kept Rose's apron tucked away, but it had also given her a great gift. Her mem had prayed. Even when Rose didn't understand, Mem had known and loved in every way possible. Had Mem's prayers carried Rose to where she was now? Rose had no doubt. Had they carried her birth parents too? Rose hoped so.

DAYS WENT BY AND ROSE DIDN'T LOOK AT THE APRON again, but every time she thought about it she realized how much that one addition to her hope chest changed everything. She'd crafted everything else in there—the linens, the towels, and the pillowcases—with care, for her future home. The apron was a reminder that those things wouldn't be used in that way. Not now.

Rose sat on one of the wooden kitchen chairs next to the

woodstove, quilting. She'd bought the fabric in the frame to create a cover for her marriage bed, but she supposed she could sell it and use it for a train ticket someplace nice. What she'd do after that she didn't know.

"Rose, would you like to play checkers with me?" Matthew asked.

Usually she would have told him maybe, after she'd quilted for a while, but now she didn't know why quilting had ever been more important than spending time with one of her siblings.

"Are you going to come to school tomorrow to read *Heidi*, Rose?" he asked. "We've missed you the last couple of weeks, and Miss Lucy said there must be something surely wrong for you not to come. I told her that I thought so too. Is there something wrong?"

Mem was in the kitchen, on her knees, with a wash pail beside her. She used a large brush to scrub with wide, sweeping motions. Each of the Yoder children had grown up pitching in and doing chores, but there was one thing Mem always did herself, and that was the kitchen floor. It was as if the sun hadn't truly set—the day done—until Mary Yoder's kitchen floor could be eaten off of with a fork.

"I can come tomorrow. I've just not been feeling well." How could she tell him that her heart was broken? She still walked through life as though she was born from Mem's womb—carried under her heart—like the rest of the children. They had no idea to suspect that after Christmas everything would change.

A hand on her shoulder caused Rose to jump. She turned to see little Martha there. "After yer game with Matthew, can you play with me?"

"*Ja, ja*, of course."

She played four games of checkers—two with each of the twins—and Mem didn't pester them when the clock ticked past their bedtimes. But the time came when the yawns and rubbing of the eyes were more frequent than not. It was then the twins put themselves to bed and Rose was forced to retreat alone to her room. That was always the hardest part of the day.

She removed her *kapp* and dressed in her bedclothes. Tonight she told herself she wouldn't wear her sleeping kerchief. What was the point? What was the point of anything?

There were moments when her mind was focused on a recipe or bathing one of the younger ones that she'd forget. Sometimes she even wanted to bring it up with her mem again, although she didn't know what she'd say. But other times, like now, she felt herself sinking into a dark place, certain she'd never feel complete peace again.

She brushed out her hair, letting it trail down her back like her mother used to do. She felt different with it down like that, braver, maybe. Just as her mom had been brave.

Rose moved to the window, pressing her fingers to the glass. Jonathan was out there somewhere, but where? Would he return if she asked? What would it hurt to add a few lines in the letter? *I miss you . . . Please come back so we can talk.* His parents would find a way to get the letter to him, wouldn't they?

Decision made, she moved to the trunk to retrieve the letter . . . but it was gone. It wasn't on the linens where she'd left it. She dug deeper, looking under every piece. It hadn't slipped underneath. Had someone knocked it out of her trunk by accident? Rose sank to her knees and looked under her bed and side table. There was nothing there. The letter was gone.

But who would have done such a thing? Who would have gotten into her—

"Elizabeth." Rose spat her sister's name. No wonder Elizabeth had had that twinkle in her eye the other day. She'd read the letter!

Without worrying about the others sleeping in the house, Rose stomped down the hall and up the stairs to Elizabeth's room. Instead of knocking, she walked right in. A candle still burned and Elizabeth was reading one of her favorite books. She jumped as Rose entered. "Rose, what's wrong? Is something the matter?"

"*Ja*, something's the matter." It took work to control her voice. "You took my letter. You read it, I just know that. How could you do that . . . get into my things?"

"You told me Nancy Shank's address was there—in your trunk. I was looking for it. I opened the letter, thinking that was the one where the address was. I didn't realize what it was until I was halfway through it. I didn't know Jonathan had left town, Rose. But the worst part was you poured out your heart and didn't give it to him. How's he supposed to come back if he doesn't know how you feel?"

"That isn't your business, now is it?"

"Vell . . . at least I'm brave enough to tell people how I feel. If I was as beautiful as you, Rose, I wouldn't hide like you do. It's almost as if you're afraid of people seeing you—even the man you love."

Rose sat on her sister's bed and closed her eyes. Now wasn't the time to raise her voice, to lash out with angry words, although they surged up inside. "Maybe I do try to hide, but I've been hurt before, you know. I don't want to face that rejection again. I wanted to send the letter, but I couldn't. What if Jonathan has already found another bride? I'd be such a fool. You can give me the letter, Elizabeth. There're a few things I want to add, and I'll think about dropping it off at Mr. and Mrs. Fisher's house, I promise."

Elizabeth bit her lip. "I can't do that. I can't give it to you."

"Yes, you can. This is not a game. It's been a long day and I'm tired . . . so very tired."

"Rose, I'm telling the truth. I can't give you the letter."

"And why not?"

"Because . . . I took it by the Fishers' place a few days ago. I told them it was from you. They seem pleased and they told me to tell you they expected Jonathan back any day now, in time for Christmas."

"You didn't . . . He's coming back?" Rose didn't know which part of Elizabeth's words she should focus on.

"Yes." Elizabeth crossed her arms over her chest. "Maybe he's here already and has read it by now."

"And do you think that's helping things? Can't I be in

charge of anything? Maybe it would be best if I leave this family. Maybe it's God's way of kicking me out the door to find my real parents."

Elizabeth's arms dropped to her side. A puzzled expression came over her face. "Rose, what are you talking about?"

Rose jutted out her chin. "If you read the letter, then you know that I'm not Amish. You know the secret, the one Mem was trying so hard to hide."

Tears tumbled from Elizabeth's eyes, and she covered her face with her hands. "*Ne*. It didn't say anything like that. You just wrote that he was special—different but special—and you loved him, and you'd find your way together. I was trying to help . . . I . . ." Elizabeth lowered her hands. "You're lying, Rose, that you're not my sister. Yer just trying to get back at me, even though I'm just trying to help."

Rose released a shuddering breath and wrapped her arms around her sister. But instead of settling into her arms, Elizabeth pulled back. She studied Rose's face. "Wait . . . you *are Englisch?*"

A lump filled Rose's throat, and she didn't know what to say. Elizabeth didn't ask for the whole story. She just continued to stare.

"I'm sorry." Elizabeth finally muttered sheepishly, as if she were talking to a schoolmate, not her sister.

"I don't blame you. You were just trying to help." Rose reached for her sister's hand and squeezed. "And yer right, I haven't been very brave lately. I'm still getting used to the truth myself."

Elizabeth cocked her head. "Do the little kids know?"

"*Ne*. And I'm dreading the day we'll have to tell them."

"Does Jonathan know?" Elizabeth asked.

"*Ja*."

Elizabeth climbed into bed and pulled the covers up, tucking into herself like a small child who was about to get disciplined. "Are you gonna leave?"

Rose shrugged. She didn't know what to say. "We can talk about it more tomorrow. I think we just both need to get some rest."

As though tending to her younger siblings, Rose tucked the blanket under Elizabeth's chin, even though she was nearly a woman, and walked to the door.

"It's sort of like *Heidi*," Elizabeth said in a sad murmur.

Rose didn't ask what she meant by that, but she knew it was true. Living one place and being drawn to another. The only thing was Heidi knew she needed to get back to her mountains, but Rose had no idea where her path would lead.

Seventeen

JONATHAN SAT AT THE SMALL CAFE IN CHARM, OHIO. He'd sat here each day for the last few weeks, talking with the locals. There were a few older families who'd known Stan and Betty Williams fifteen years prior. He'd chatted with most of them, but no one had heard much from the *Englisch* family after they left.

One woman—a schoolteacher in Berlin—knew of the couple. She'd been the first one who'd opened up. She'd even driven him to Charm that first day in her car. She'd also said that her friend had been the midwife for both Rose's and Daisy's births. The midwife had been out of town, but now she'd returned. Jonathan prayed he'd find answers. This was his last hope.

He wanted to give this gift to Rose. More than anything he wanted to be the one who helped heal her heart. He'd been staying with a cousin in Charm, but recently he'd returned to Berlin to check on his parents and to look over their finances at the end of the year, since they always counted on him for that. That's when he found Rose's letter waiting. His heartbeat quickened even now.

She wanted to try to forge ahead and create a future with him. The least he could do was attempt to bring some solace into her past.

He tapped his fingers on the yellow Formica tabletop and then stood when he saw an older Amish woman entering. She leaned heavily on her cane. Her gray hair was pulled tight at the center part.

"I DELIVERED THOSE GIRLS AND EVEN THOUGH I'M Amish and Betty was *Englisch*, she became my best friend. She was such a beautiful, creative soul," the woman confessed to him over a cup of coffee and pie.

"Did you hear from her after they moved?"

"Around once a year, usually around Christmas. And then there was one year . . . there were so many letters. At least one a week. Betty was worried about Rose. She feared something had happened to her. I wrote to reassure her. The Yoders lived in Berlin then. They'd moved not many months after frail, blonde Rose became a part of their family. Even though Berlin seems like a world away from Charm, I made sure to keep track of the family. A few people in Charm talked about the way she was abandoned—those things do create a buzz at first—but soon it just became part of life. I don't believe the secret followed them when they left, and in our minds we felt it was better to just keep the matter to ourselves."

Jonathan nodded. "And after that?"

"After a while Betty seemed content yet. She had peace over her decision. I'm not sure if it was something I'd said in my letters that reassured her, or maybe my prayers helped even more."

The woman reached down and pulled something out of her pocket. "Every year Betty sent me a letter. They stopped for a number of years, and I was worried. But this note explains what happened." The woman smiled. "If you notice the return address is in Columbus—not far from here. There's no number to call, but maybe you can call information? I have an *Englisch* neighbor with a phone. I'm sure she can help you with that."

Jonathan wanted to leap from his seat. Instead he reached over and patted the woman's hand. "Thank you . . . thank you so much. I have to say you've jest given me the best Christmas gift ever."

"I hope it turns out well—your plan, that is." The woman smiled.

Jonathan had only three more days to make his dreams—Rose's unspoken wish—come true before Christmas.

MEM DIDN'T THINK ANYTHING OF ROSE ASKING TO TAKE the buggy. She drove it to the school to read from the book *Heidi*. As Rose sat on the stool in front of the children, their curious gazes pierced her. She supposed she'd stare, too, if she saw a grown woman tearing up as she read a book. But the tears couldn't be held back as she read the familiar words:

"'Where is the child?'" Rose read. "Heidi was fetched, and as she walked up to him to say, 'Good morning,' he looked inquiringly into her face and said, 'Well, what do you say to this, little one?'

"Heidi looked at him in perplexity."

"'Why, you don't know anything about it, I see,' laughed Herr Sesemann. 'You are going home today, going at once.'"

"'Home,' murmured Heidi in a low voice, turning pale; she was so overcome that for a moment or two she could hardly breathe."

Rose thought of those words as she finished up with the class, and she realized she couldn't wait until after Christmas after all to talk to Curtis. Why wait? Why continue to live with the questions . . . the ache of the heart? She thought about the words from the book all the way to Hummel's Grocery. If Curtis was who she thought he was, she would find *home* today—or at least part of it.

Rose stamped her feet to keep them warm as she waited for Mrs. Miller to open the front door of her grocery after taking off time for lunch. The shop was a few minutes late opening . . . not that it mattered. For so long, during the war, it seemed like all they did was wait. Wait for news to trickle down to their community like a slow-moving stream. Wait for the items they needed to fill the store shelves.

Being pacifists, the war didn't change the Amish community much. Men worked at the jobs they'd always worked—at least most did. Mothers cared for children and for their home. Children went to school and did the evening chores.

Yet everything had been different too.

Banners with gold stars hung in the windows of some

Englisch homes. The banners meant that a son had died in the war. The *Englisch* grief at times turned into anger against those in her Amish community.

"To say you're against the war is to say you're against my son," Mrs. Miller had declared to Dat one warm, summer afternoon, the same day they'd heard about the American landing at Normandy. *"How can you live in peace when we're sacrificing everything?"*

Live in peace? Is that really how the world saw things? *Ja*, their Amish sons didn't fight—well, at least not most of them—but what Rose carried inside didn't feel peaceful at all. Sometimes the hardest war was the one unknown to others, fought in one's own soul.

Finally, Mrs. Miller strode to the front and opened the door. Even though a cold wind blew down the back of her neck, Rose stood just outside the door and watched Curtis hauling two large crates, filled with canned goods, from the back. He set them down in one of the aisles and then pulled his kerchief out of his pants pocket, wiping his brow.

Seeing him, she didn't know how everyone couldn't see the resemblance—or how she had missed it before. He had the same light hair, fair skin, and a splattering of freckles across his nose. And their eyes . . . When she looked into Curtis's eyes she saw the same milky-blue color that she'd noticed in her reflection in her hand mirror at home.

Unable to stand still anymore, Rose tucked her hands into her coat pockets and strode in his direction. He was squatted down, carefully lining up rows of green beans on the shelf.

Hearing her footsteps, he glanced up and his eyes lit up. "Rose!"

"Can we talk?"

"Do you need me to find something? Maybe on one of the shelves? Or . . ." He cocked his head. "Maybe you already found something, Rose? Something you'd like to talk to me about?"

"*Ja*." She nodded. "I was thinking we'd talk about more personal things, Curtis. Like our family."

He straightened then, standing over her by at least six inches. Yet by the look on his face it seemed he was a little boy who'd just been caught sneaking a cookie.

"You could have told me . . . weeks ago. You should have said you were my brother and whatnot."

Curtis's lips pressed into a taut line. He didn't deny it. He didn't apologize. Instead he simply nodded once. "I just had my lunch break, but I can see if Mrs. Miller can cover for me . . . since it's an emergency."

"Please, would you?" She covered her mouth with her hand. Her fingers were trembling. "I'd appreciate that. I can meet you at the cafe next door."

She turned and strode out the door, trying not to run. *Why didn't I ask more? Why didn't I ask him what he remembers?* Did Curtis have any idea that what happened then impacted so much now? She might never get married. She'd be *maidel* forever.

"He didn't deny he was my brother," Rose mumbled to herself as she made her way down the sidewalk. It was strange to realize that what she was looking for had been right in front of her the whole time. What answers would he give? And was it possible that this first reunion would lead to many more?

IT ONLY TOOK A FEW MINUTES FOR CURTIS TO JOIN Rose at the Country Cafe next door. They sat in a back booth. A couple of Amish womenfolk enjoying bowls of soup glared at Rose. Most likely because of her connection with Jonathan and his serving in the military. And now to be seen in public with an *Englisch*man . . . *"The shame of it,"* she imagined them thinking.

One of those popular, upbeat songs on the radio ended with the announcer's excited voice talking about the Nazi doctors put on trial in Nuremberg, Germany. Rose knew a radio announcer wouldn't be needed for everyone in her community to know she'd had lunch with an *Englisch*man. Rose guessed Dat, Mem, and everyone up and down their country road would know by supper, since these women knew her parents well.

She leaned forward, resting her arms on the table and giving Curtis her full attention. Who cared what those women thought? When the truth of who she really was came out, this lunch would seem like a small thing.

"I s'pose I should apologize." Curtis fiddled with the napkin on the table. "I wanted to tell you, but you seemed so happy. I wasn't sure if you knew."

"I didn't know. Not until recently. It was very much a surprise," she said. "I have to say, though, that my parents—my Amish parents—gave me a *gut* home."

Curtis lowered his head. His finger traced a mar on the tabletop, and she could tell that he'd wished he could have done more to help his parents from having to let her go.

"Can you tell me about it . . . what you remember?" Her words caught as she spoke them.

"I remember that day. It was cold, real cold, but nothing as chilling as my mother's wailings as the train carried us away from Ohio. We'd gotten to somewhere in Nevada when she woke up with a start one night and started running down the aisle of the train. I'll never forget her wailing as long as I live. 'Rose, Rose.' Dad chased her, but she didn't want to listen when he reminded her of where she—where you—were. And why they left you. Mama was quiet the rest of the way after that. Her face was ashen gray, the same color as the coat she wore. The same color as the morning they found little Daisy gone.

"When we got to California, things got worse instead of better. It seemed as if she thought of you—cared for you—even more than she wished to care for us. Then, one day, everything changed. I heard Mama singing—just under her breath. I felt all warm inside hearing it, even though our little house was so cold. Dad asked her about it later. I think he was afraid to at the time, and Mama said that she'd had a dream. You were older and beautiful, happy and healthy, running through the fields behind the Yoder house. She was so happy watching you, and as you ran over a ridge she turned and realized that someone was standing beside her. It was a man with gentle eyes and a happy smile. He said that you were going to have a good life. He told Mama you would be all right."

Rose studied Curtis's face, unsure if she understood what he was telling her. Questions throbbed in her head, and her thick wool coat captured her heartbeat.

"She missed you, Rose. Christmas was always the hardest time for years to come. But whenever she talked to you she said that you were 'under Jesus's eye.' If I heard that phrase one time, I heard it one hundred."

A tingling sensation moved down Rose's neck, into her chest, and her breathing became labored, as if the air had grown as thick as chocolate pudding. What did that mean? She lived a Plain, normal life. Rose had neither exceptional beauty nor any specific talent. She had no intentions to do anything grand with her life. Her greatest dream was marrying Jonathan and having a family of her own. If Jesus's eye was on her, He certainly had to be disappointed.

Rose fidgeted slightly, and Curtis ordered two cups of coffee and two of the daily specials before continuing.

"Dad found work in Alameda, working for the telephone company—setting poles, of all things. Things got better, eventually."

"Can you tell me about something else? About Daisy."

"*Ja*. She died just shy of her second birthday. She was never well, couldn't gain weight. Wherever Mama went in

Charm, ladies said Daisy looked like a little china doll, mostly because she just sat in her stroller so quiet and still, unlike us boys, who never stopped running."

"It's so sad that our mother lost . . . both girls."

He nodded. "Mama went into a dark place after Daisy died. And then you got sick, Rose. You were in a mighty bad spot. I'd watch you all the time, sure you'd be gone next. Mama couldn't deal with it. That's when the nightmares came. She dreamt that she went to Daisy's grave and when she looked down at the headstone it was your name on it. It was Dad who suggested that they leave you with the Yoders. They were much better off than us. Our parents knew you'd be cared for . . . that you'd no doubt soon have your health back."

"But why didn't they just ask? Why did they leave me that way?"

Curtis shrugged. "Shame, I suppose. No one likes to feel he or she failed their family . . ."

Rose released a soft sigh, wondering what she'd do, thankful they cared enough to sacrifice their hearts.

"Mama wrote many letters back to Charm—to a friend she knew—and the news was all the same: you were fine. She read them over dinner, and the peace came again after that. Mama decided she didn't want to disrupt you. She turned to God and even had two more children—twin boys, Bobby and Rodney.

"It was that year that Dad came home with a special Christmas present for Mama—a Christmas rose. And every year that was her favorite Christmas gift."

He paused his story, eating the turkey and rice with large bites.

"It's so hard to take everything in . . . but are they doing all right? Daddy, Mama, and the boys? Although I suppose the twins must be teenagers now, *ja*? Maybe around the age of my sister Elizabeth." A smiled filled Rose's face at the thought.

Curtis paused with the fork halfway to his lips. "Oh, I'm sorry. Maybe I should have started with that. They're gone, Rose, both Dad and Mama. She died after a bad illness right before the war. And Dad died of pneumonia just six months after that. I was in boot camp when I got the news. All our brothers—well, I wish I could tell you where they ended up. When I left for the war Bobby and Rodney were still in high school. Timothy was working as a flight instructor in Texas. We didn't do a great job writing—most guys don't. When I sent a dozen letters and all of them returned, I called the school and they said the boys finished up early and they and Timothy had moved to work for a transportation company. Instead of returning to California I headed here. It's always seemed more like home to me, even though I was just a little kid when we left. But mostly I wanted to see you." He smiled. "I wish Mama was around so I could tell her it's true. God's hand has been on you."

Rose sat there a moment, letting the news sink in. Her parents—both parents were gone. She'd never meet them. She'd never get to hear their side of the story. She pushed the plate away, sure she couldn't take one more bite.

"There is one more thing, Rose, that you need to know."

She looked at her brother. The compassion was clear on his face.

"I also came because Mom asked that whenever I had a chance I'd come check on you. She had letters from friends, but she wanted me to see for myself."

"Thank you." Rose reached over and took his hand, then forced a smile. "I appreciate you telling me. More than that, though, I appreciate you coming."

"I like it here, Rose. It's a good place. I can see it becoming home."

Home. Heidi had returned home, but now Rose would never have the chance. Not the home she hoped to find with her father and mother, at least.

"If possible, I'd like to get to know the Yoders better. Without knowing where our brothers are, well, you're the only family I have left."

Rose's lower lip trembled and suddenly she felt like a fool. She'd been so wrapped up in her feelings that she hadn't thought about Curtis—a veteran, a good man. He didn't have a family to return to after the war.

A true smile filled her face this time. She squeezed her brother's hand. "I know Mem and Dat will love it. And I will too. I'm looking forward to getting to know you better. To spend time with you."

Curtis glanced down at his watch, gasped, and then stood. He put enough money on the table for the bill and turned to her. "I need to get back or I'm not going to have a job to return to."

He took two steps, then turned and offered an impromptu hug. She laughed and realized that even though she hadn't been born Amish, she was raised to think like one—and hugging wasn't something you'd ever do in public. Still, she smiled and returned the embrace. Rose knew that in the months and years to come, merging two lifestyles would take some getting used to.

Curtis waved and walked out the door, and again Rose saw the eyes of the Amish women on her. It didn't matter if they disapproved. Like a jigsaw puzzle, a few pieces of her heart connected in a way they never had before.

Eighteen

THE SNOW FELL HEAVILY THE DAY BEFORE CHRISTMAS and even though Curtis had been over to get to know her family, Rose couldn't make herself truly get into the Christmas spirit. In just a month's time she discovered parents, and now mourned their loss. In a month's time she'd seen Jonathan again, and had hoped for a renewed relationship, but the days had passed and still he was nowhere to be seen. She'd even gone to church in hopes of seeing him but was disappointed. And now she sat with Mem and Mrs. Ault, sipping cups of tea and trying to pretend her mind was on their conversation and not on the man she loved.

Wrinkles furrowed Mrs. Ault's brow. She'd chatted with Mem about quilting and canning, but Rose could see it was the last thing she wanted to talk about. Finally, the older woman got around to what was really on her heart.

"Harold is living half in the past, half in the present." Mrs. Ault sighed. "I just wish he'd pick one. Sometimes he acts as if yesterday was the battle. But then, in the beat of a heart, he's with us. He's present, aware of his splintered mind. That's the hardest part—seeing him embarrassed and unsure of his future. Days pass, and he's sleeping more and more. I wonder if it's because it's acceptable to be unable to control a dream, but the worst dreams are the ones you're awake for and still can't control."

As Mrs. Ault continued, Rose stood to retrieve more water for hot tea. The pounding of the door caused her to jump. She hurried over and opened it. There stood Mr. Ault panting, his eyes wild.

"It's Harold. I fell asleep on the couch and woke realizing an hour passed and he was gone. I've searched the house and the barn. He isn't anywhere. I looked for footprints in the snow, but the only ones came here. I took the liberty of looking in your barn . . . He's not there." His eyes were wide and she could see his heartbeat pounding in his temple.

"Please come in. We can make a plan. Could we maybe ask the neighbors to help?"

Mr. Ault reluctantly agreed and then entered. His shoulders slumped and his gaze turned to his wife. "I'm so sorry. I shouldn't have let myself fall asleep—"

"It's not your fault." Mrs. Ault hurried toward him. "We'll find him. It'll be okay." She patted her husband's arm, then turned to Rose. "Do you think you can go . . . go ask some of the neighbors if—"

"No." The word shot from Rose's mouth. "I—I think I know where he is." She hurriedly slipped on her snow boots and reached for her coat and scarf. "The old springhouse. We'd go there—Harold, Marcus, Vera, and I. We'd hide in there and tell stories. We'd see how long we could last after day turned to dusk, and we'd tell ourselves we were brave. If his footprints came this way, I think that is where he would go."

She moved to the door.

Mr. Ault stepped forward. "I'll go with you."

Rose held up a hand. "No, please. If he is there I'd like to talk to him . . . just me and him." Mr. Ault looked unsure. "If he's not I'll be back immediately, I promise."

Rose glanced at Mem, who looked worried. Rose slipped out the door into the cool mid-morning air before her mother had a chance to change her mind.

The old springhouse was just a little past the barn, amid a cluster of trees. There was a small gulley that dipped down where the creek used to run. After moving to the property her dat had diverted the creek to better water the fields and gardens and had built a new springhouse. They used that to keep butter, milk, and other items cool during the summer months. The old one had become a playhouse.

When she rounded the barn Rose tried to think of what to say, but no words came. About twenty feet away she paused, knowing it wouldn't be a good idea to startle Harold. "Harold? Hey, there . . . It's me, Rose," she called. "Is there room enough in there for me to join you?"

There was no sound, no movement at first. Then, ever so slowly, the door opened halfway. Rose took that as her sign to enter. She approached, hunched over. The first thing that hit her was the damp, musty smell in the dim area. The second was the sound of Harold blowing his nose into his handkerchief.

"If we were playing hide-and-seek, I just won." She tried to keep her tone light. "Yer dat . . . he was looking all over, but I knew where you'd be."

He was sitting on the dirt floor. "I feel so stupid."

Rose looked around, knowing her only option was to join him on the ground. She sat, and though the earth was cold at least it was dry.

"Next time you'll jest have to hide better. Maybe up in the loft." Rose chuckled.

"You know what I'm talking about, Rose. I'm out of my mind and everyone knows it."

"You've been through trauma, Harold. You'll get better."

"I wish I could hope for that."

She patted his hand. "You can pray about it."

Harold shook his head. "Don't you think I have?"

Rose pressed her lips together. She understood. She'd prayed a lot too—for her parents, for Jonathan—but that didn't mean her prayers did any good.

"What's going to happen with me, Rose? Am I going to live the rest of my life counting on my parents? There are times I know that what I'm saying doesn't make sense, but the images are so real. The emotions are so real."

"Things like that are hard to shake off, like a tick on a hound."

He nodded but didn't answer.

"Things haven't been easy on me lately either," she finally

admitted. "I found out news about my parents—my biological ones. Did you know about them?"

Harold nodded slowly. "Yeah. I heard your mom and my mom talking once. I wasn't supposed to hear. I brought it up that night at dinner and Dad told me if I said a word I'd get the switching of my life."

"Well, you did a good job keeping the secret, then. It's sad, really, thinking that I had to be rescued like that. Knowing that my parents' greatest act of love was giving me over to another family, in order to save my life."

He nodded and fiddled with the shoestrings on his boots. Rose didn't know if he was listening or not, but at least it felt good to know that truth about what he'd heard too.

"I suppose that's what you were talking about."

"Excuse me?"

"When I brought you that apple pie you said when you were on the beach and you knew God was protecting you, just as He protected me. Well, you said you thought about me and my rescue. That's what you meant, wasn't it?"

"I did think of you, Rose, but you got it wrong. When I was on that beach I didn't think about the fact the Yoders rescued you—although that was true too. I thought about how you'd rescued them."

Rose's eyebrows furrowed. "What do you mean?"

"When I overheard, Rose, it was your mom that was talking. She said that she and your dad had been going through a hard time. She questioned everything about her faith and marriage. She said she felt as if she was living with a stranger and she had a very hard heart. And then . . . you came."

"I don't understand—what does that have to do with anything?"

"Well, from what I remembered—I was only a kid—she'd prayed to God and asked for a miracle to show her that what she was devoting her life to mattered. She also saw your dad in a new light. He was so kind and compassionate with you—a child not his own. Seeing the way he held you as you cried, and the way he played with you to get your mind off of missing your family, made her fall in love with him all over again."

A warmth filled Rose's chest and moved through her body. "That's amazing . . . I had no idea. I was Mem's miracle," she said more to herself than to him. She pondered that for a while, sitting in the childhood playhouse with her childhood friend. "But what did that have to do with your battle on the beach?"

"Oh, Rose, that's easy." Harold smiled. "I remembered that when God gives us more than we can handle it is also possible that a miracle will soon be walking our way. All we have to do is pray."

Rose reached over and took Harold's hand, squeezing it tight. "In that case, do you mind if I pray?"

Harold lowered his head. "I don't mind."

"Dear Lord . . ." Rose cleared her throat.

Harold's head lifted again. "Out loud?"

Rose smiled. "*Ja*. Don't tell anyone, but my mem has

often prayed out loud. I learned from her. I find it easier to keep my mind focused on God, don't you?"

Instead of answering, Harold lowered his head again.

"Dear Lord, we come to You now, and even though we don't always reveal our inside needs, we are often in need of courage. For both Harold and me, we ache for our past, and our future seems so uncertain. Would You be with us now? Would You help us be brave? And mostly, would You bring a miracle? I have no idea what that looks like, but I know that in both of our cases we need to look down the road and trust in faith. Help us to have faith. Amen."

The words were simple, but an electric current moved through her body, and it felt as if her words were truly heard. With a smile at Harold, she stood and moved to the door of the old springhouse. "Do you want to come to the house?"

Harold nodded. "Thank you, Rose." It was just a simple phrase. "Thank you for reminding me that the future is in God's hands."

"You're welcome. And remember, wherever you go, in body and mind, you simply need to call out to God and He is there."

Back at the house, relief filled the faces of Mr. and Mrs. Ault. Harold entered and looked around, as if numerous memories came flooding back. Yet part of him also looked tired, and the Aults regretfully cut short their visit. As she watched them leave, Rose was thankful that the kids were in school and Dat was in the barn. Rose tried to picture who Mem had been fifteen years ago. Mem seemed so settled in her life, but obviously there were many things that had happened over the years to make that so.

Rose poured another cup of tea for each of them and sat. "Mr. and Mrs. Ault looked pretty worried." She took a sip.

"*Ja*, I feel bad for them. I wish I could do more. It's so hard . . ."

"Dat says it's harder to see your children suffering than suffer yourself. I'm sorry that I caused you so many days of concern too. Some days I feel like Heidi, in the book, going through the motions but longing for my real home. I've been living with a splintered mind, Mem, like Harold—half here and half there. I'm ready to choose now. To focus on the place I'm meant to be forever, even if I've never been there before." Rose offered a sad smile. "But I have to trust in what I cannot see, isn't that what you've always said?"

"*Ja*, Rose. It's the definition of faith. Faith doesn't pay attention to our worries; it looks beyond what we can't see. What one thinks, feels, doesn't matter. Your deeds don't give faith no mind. It's all on Jesus. It's trusting He will be there even when we step out to an unknown place."

"That's exactly how I feel, Mem. As if I'm stepping out into the unknown."

Mem's chin quivered as she heard those words. "So does that mean you've made your decision? Yer leaving to find your family?"

"*Ach*, no. Didn't you know? This is my home. Those fields are my Heidi mountains. And the community . . . They'll have to accept my differences, just as I'll learn to accept theirs." Then, through a thin film of tears, she winked at her mother. "And you, Mem, are my grandfather."

The shaking of Mem's shoulders was the first response, and then a cry—a happy cry—escaped out of her mouth. "Oh, Rose." Mem rose and hurried to her. Rose stood and allowed herself to be engulfed in her mother's arms. "That's so good to know. I've tried not to pressure you."

"I know, Mem." Rose's cheek rubbed against her mem's *kapp* as they embraced. "You haven't. I've just been reminded today that one never knows what's in store, right down the road."

Nineteen

CHRISTMAS MORNING DAWNED, AND WITH IT ROSE FELT a renewed sense of thankfulness to God. Even though a part of her heart mourned for what she'd lost, the majority of what she felt was gratitude for where God placed her.

If only I could talk to Jonathan again—to tell him that I was learning to trust. And learning better to be trustworthy.

For many weeks Rose had thought it was her parents who made the decision to leave her with the Yoders, but had God directed them? God knew the times. The struggles of simple people. He'd given her not one set of parents, but two. Two sets of parents who loved her. He'd given her brothers and sisters. A community. God had given her His love, and the love of Jonathan.

And as they gathered for Christmas dinner she just wished she had a way to find Jonathan and tell him. Even with all the faces of her family—and Curtis—who would soon be gathering around the dinner table, not having the man she loved there made the whole day incomplete.

Rose sighed as she plunged the metal masher into her potatoes. *Dear God, if there is even the chance for me to see*

Jonathan again . . . to talk to him again . . . to really share my heart, I'll take it. If ever . . .

Vera approached with baby Ira on her hip. "I see you have your apron on. It's beautiful. I love those yellow roses."

"Thank you. I like it, too, and Dat didn't even say anything about it being *fancy*."

"Do the little ones know?" Vera dipped her finger into the potatoes and put a clump in her mouth. Then she turned and looked out the window, something catching her attention.

"Not yet. Mem and I plan on telling them soon." Rose glanced over her shoulder to where Curtis was telling them about the orchards and beaches in California. "The kids like Curtis. I think they'll be happy to know he's a permanent fixture in our family."

"And it looks like he might not be the only one." Vera winked.

Rose followed Vera's gaze and her heart jumped into her throat to see Jonathan stepping onto the porch. Without a word she rushed to the door and tugged it open. She pushed aside the screen and before she knew it she was in Jonathan's arms.

His chest vibrated with his chuckle. "*Ja*, that's some sort of welcome. And I'd had a long apology speech all planned."

Rose stepped back slightly, embarrassed for her display of affection. She turned back, noticing all eyes upon her—especially Curtis's. She knew she'd have to explain, but her brother could wait. She just wanted to soak in the fact that Jonathan was here—that he'd come.

She motioned to the living room. "Won't you come in?"

"Actually, can you come out . . . just for a few minutes? I went through all the trouble of memorizing my thoughts. Do you think you could hear me out?"

"*Ja.*" Rose stepped in just briefly and put on her boots and her coat. And as Mem advised the children to "not gawk so or you'll get no dessert," she stepped out to the man of her dreams—her good dreams—sitting there in the swing with a smile that could not be ignored.

"Rose, I know you said that things could never work between us. You said you couldn't offer yourself when you didn't know who you were. But I'm not going to stand for that. You—of anyone—should know that when I believe in something I'm going to give my all to it. I believe in us, Rose. When I first returned I questioned if maybe you were right . . . that I didn't fit in this community. That we could never have a place here together. You made me start to doubt, but I don't worry anymore, especially when I received your letter."

"You're not concerned that I'm not Amish?" she had to ask one more time.

"I told you, you are as much Amish as anyone in this community. The foundation of our faith is to love God with everything and to live united in this community. You felt like you didn't belong because you weren't born Amish. I might have rightly lost my place because I chose to do things the *Englisch* way. But it's God—not man—who's our judge. A God who offers forgiveness. A God who sets those who may feel solitary in families, who brings out those who are bound in chains, whether it be chains from others or their own feelings of unworthiness—"

"You're saying a lot, Jonathan." She grinned up at him. "But I'm still waiting to see what you're getting at."

"You're right. I'm talking too much. It's better to show you, because they might be a bit chilled."

Rose's eyebrows peaked. "They?"

"Come, I have something to show you."

Rose stood, and with one motion Jonathan wrapped her scarf around her neck and knotted it. Then he took her hand and led her down the porch steps.

His buggy stood parked near the barn. There were people out there too. Men. *Englisch*men.

She approached, noting that there was something familiar about them. White-blond hair. Long faces. Large blue eyes. The men looked like Curtis . . . Like her.

Rose paused. Her heart pounded and her knees softened to jelly. And yet it felt like more puzzle pieces slid into place and more segments of her life seemed to make sense.

The men stood there with smiles, yet instead of rushing toward her they waited for her to approach. She needed to take the steps. As with any relationship, one had to step toward it. And to do so one had to be sure of who she was first. One had to know what she had to offer.

"How did this happen?" Her voice wasn't much louder than a whisper.

"I found a friend of your mother's, Rose. She pointed the way."

"Wait!" Rose turned and hurried back to the front door, ignoring Jonathan's puzzled expression. She pushed the door open, and it flung wide to hit the wall. "Curtis, come! Come!" She didn't wait to see if he was going to follow, but quickly returned to Jonathan's side.

Instead of heading over to the waiting men, Jonathan turned to her.

"Rose Yoder, I want to marry you, and I wanted you to step into our union sure of who you are. Sure of the community. Sure of your place in it. I hope you choose to stay Amish, but if not, I'm not so fearful of the *Englisch* world as I used to be."

"So you did this? You found my family?"

"I didn't want you committing your life to me with your mind full of questions. I know the pain of that. I've seen it."

"Jonathan, I . . ." Did she have all the answers she needed? What had God been showing her? Even without her family, without Jonathan, God was enough.

He turned and began walking again.

Rose took his hand and her feet propelled her forward. There was no hesitancy as she strode up to the strangers. They all looked similar to Curtis, to her. Her brothers. She paused only to look to Jonathan. He'd done this, for her. She saw it now—the clear love in his eyes that her sister Vera had described. He did love her—more than she could ever grasp. His love had propelled him to leave her for a time in order to give her the greatest gift.

"*Danki*," she mouthed.

Jonathan nodded and smiled.

Then Rose turned back to her brothers. One of the twins looked to the others, and then he pulled something from behind his back. It was a red flower with a long stem.

Her fingers fluttered to her lips. "A rose."

Then, one by one, the other brothers revealed their same offering.

"Christmas roses." Curtis's joyful voice came from behind. Then he walked around and huddled his brothers up in a firm embrace.

When they turned back around they wore happy, matching expressions. Curtis made introductions to Rose—Timothy and the twins, Bobby and Rodney.

He smiled at the roses his brothers held. "Just like Mom received every Christmas, to remind her—us—of you."

"I can't imagine a more wonderful gift." The tears came again.

"We haven't just come for a visit, Rose. It seems Jonathan also has plans for an Amish wedding." Timothy smiled.

"I like that thought." She gazed up at her future husband. "Very, very much."

Rose heard the crunching of footsteps on the snow behind her. She turned as Marcus approached from behind, nodding his head in agreement. "It's about time. That's all I've got to say!" He introduced himself to Rose's brothers.

Brothers. What could be more wonderful than brothers?

Jonathan cleared his throat. "I'm not sure these roses

will last until then, but we found some greenhouses nearby to get more."

"But roses at an Amish wedding? It seems so fancy." She chuckled.

"But it seems right for someone like our Rose," Rodney said.

As Rose stood there, Bobby approached her first. He handed his rose to her. Then Timothy, followed by Rodney.

"Our dad and mom . . . they would want nothing more than to have been here with you," Timothy said, "celebrating the life and love that God has given you." He peered over her shoulder. "Can we meet them—meet the other part of your family?"

With Jonathan beside her, Rose led the way inside. Tears filled her eyes as she noticed that Mem had added small candles to the greenery in the windows. It had just started to get dark, and already the numerous candles had a familiar glow.

The Christmas season was upon her, but the feelings of pain and longing were gone. Rose had been given a great gift—not only one family to love her, but two. And now, with Jonathan by her side, she'd have her own family to love. She'd have children someday, and a good community to raise them in. Not a perfect community, but one she'd learn to accept as they'd learn to accept her—to accept them.

Rose knew the story she would tell her children someday. The story about her helping to rescue the Yoders and about being rescued herself not only by a loving Amish family, but also by God. That was the most important part. No matter where she went, God was her family. He was her hope. For a while she'd thought she'd been stripped of so much, but now she knew she'd been given everything she ever needed.

Rose squeezed Jonathan's hand. She'd been given a love—many loves—that would last forever. She twirled the rose in her fingers, feeling for the first time that she'd finally found home.

Home.

Author's Note

In 2011 my friend Twyla and I visited Pennsylvania and Ohio, touring the beautiful Amish communities along the way. One night we had dinner with three Amish couples. We asked about their lives and their faith. They asked about ours. We laughed and shared. It was a rich time indeed. I was full—both from the buffet of food and the conversations.

And then, in parting, I heard a story that piqued my interest. It was about the grandmother of one of the men. During the Depression his grandmother (a child at the time) often found friendship—and food—at the house of her Amish neighbors. And then one day she returned home after a day of play to find her *Englisch* family gone. They'd left her—not because of displeasure, but because they wanted her to have a life they couldn't give.

From that story this one was born. History is worth delving into. I was blessed to be able to do so! What family story do you have to listen to or to share?

Tricia Goyer
Little Rock, Arkansas
2013

Discussion Questions

1. In *A Christmas Gift for Rose*, Rose is angry at the man she'd planned on marrying, Jonathan Fisher, because he left their Amish community to serve in the military. Why did this make Rose angry? Was it justifiable?
2. Even as Rose thinks there is no hope for her and Jonathan because of his closeness with the *Englisch* during the war, she discovers she's *Englisch* herself. What conflicts does this bring in Rose's heart?
3. Jonathan's sister Ruthann urges him to risk his heart. Why is it tough for him to step out again?
4. Rose knew that any compromise against their Amish traditions would lead to more compromise, and soon one would no longer be Amish. Do you ever feel pulled by following your parents' traditions and creating your own? How?
5. During World War II most Amishmen chose to join the Conservation Corp or spend their time in jail or working on farms. How did the war impact these men and those in their community?

6. Even though Rose was an adult she wished she could crawl onto her father's lap and let him rock her. Do you think Rose's closeness to her Amish parents made it harder or easier on her when she discovered the truth?
7. Rose had to trust God and depend on Him more when she felt her whole world torn apart. How has God met you in your dark times?
8. In addition to Jonathan and Rose coming to terms with their new lives, Rose's neighbor Harold also had to deal with returning home after the war. How were Rose and Jonathan able to help Harold?
9. Rose received a few special gifts at the end of the book. How do you think those gifts help Rose find "home"?

Acknowledgments

THIS STORY WOULD NOT HAVE HAPPENED EXCEPT FOR wonderful booksellers Eli and Vesta Hochstetler of The Gospel Store (www.mygospelbookstore.com) in Berlin, Ohio who set up a wonderful dinner with three amazing Amish couples. It was a night of great conversation and stories. I'm forever grateful to Eli and Vesta and those couples!

Thank you to Amy Lathrop and the Litfuze Hens, Caitlin Wilson, Audra Jennings, and Christen Krumm for supporting me and helping me stay connected with my readers . . . and for the gazillion other things you do!

I appreciate the Zondervan/HarperCollins Christian Publishing Team: Sue Brower, Daisy Hutton, Bridget Klein, Becky Monds, Katie Bond, and Laura Dickerson. Also thank you, Leslie Peterson, for your great editing! I also send thanks to all the unsung heroes: the managers, designers, copy editors, sales people, financial folks, etc. who make a book possible.

I'm also thankful for my agent, Janet Grant. Your help, inspiration, and guidance are priceless.

And I'm thankful for my family:

John, my wonderful husband, and our kids (and grandkids!): Cory, Katie, Clayton, and Chloe. Leslie, Nathan, Bella, Alyssa, and Casey! Also, Nathan, Kayleigh, MaCayla, Audrie-Onna, and Donovan. What an amazing family.

Grandma Dolores, your love and laughter brighten my day.

Finally, God, for adopting me into Your forever family.

With her heart—and her loyalty—on the line, can she let true love in her life?

Available in print and e-book